The Problem with Janice

A Case for Crabbe and Crabbe

Geoffrey Foster

July 2011

Geoffrey Foster was born in London, England in 1933, and his childhood was mostly spent in the County of Kent, in southeast England. Some of the action of this book, which has occasional echoes of his own experiences, takes place in or around that area and in the suburbs of London.

His father was a policeman most of his working life, and his mother, when she worked, was a shorthand typist (a stenographer). He has two sisters, five and thirteen years younger than himself.

He went to public elementary and secondary school and then to the University of Cambridge, where he studied engineering. Moving to Australia in 1959, he taught Mechanical Engineering at the University of Queensland for 14 years, before switching to educational development, running workshops and other activities for academics. Eventually he took early retirement in 1995.

As well as writing, he likes reading, listening to music, solving cryptic crosswords, walking the family beagle, Kafka, and playing a game with his younger sister, Ynes, that they whimsically refer to as 'tennis.'

Also by Geoffrey Foster:

Kit and the Beeman   ISBN 978-0-9805310-0-8

Kit the Venturer   ISBN 978-0-9805310-1-5

Vincent the Beeman   ISBN 978-0-9805310-2-2

Beatrice's Birthday   ISBN 978-0-9805310-3-9

Beatrice and Vincent's Welsh Adventures

                              ISBN 978-0-9805310-4-6

Trouble at the Mill: A Case for Crabbe and Crabbe

                              ISBN 978-0-9805310-6-0

But is it Art?: A Case for Crabbe and Crabbe

                              ISBN 978-0-9805310-7-7

This book:

The Problem with Janice: A Case for Crabbe and Crabbe

                              ISBN 978-0-9805310-8-4

Chapter 1

Nobody at the Woodhampton Castle Hotel woke up particularly early on the Sunday morning after the grand party, which had gone on until all hours. The guest of honour, the newly-promoted Detective-Inspector Jimmy Manley, had faded much earlier in the evening, having spent an energetic day at the beach helping his wife and children build sand-castles.

Melpomene Crabbe managed to stagger out of bed around half-past eight, take a bath and ring for coffee and the papers, and when the maid brought them she shook Alex awake, "Rise and shine, darling! Crabbe and Crabbe has work to do before we drive back to London!"

"What work would that be, Mel? I thought we had decided that our last case could safely be left to the police and the courts to clear up, didn't we? Or have some of those art-dealing villains popped their heads up again?"

"No, Alex, I'm referring to what Phoebe Buckmaster was asking me about yesterday – you know, her concerns about her school-friend, Janice. I don't know whether or not this is really a case for our detective agency, but I feel obliged to put some effort into it – she is a family friend after all – at least, her father, Major Buckmaster, is."

"Yes," said Alex, "I was chatting to Stephen between courses at dinner and he was complaining that the life of a country magistrate seems very boring now, with none of Crabbe and Crabbe's customers to liven the place up! All he is getting is a succession of drunk and disorderly weavers and farmhands and a few speed hogs or shop lifters, with hardly a shooting, a poisoning or a kidnapping to break the monotony!"

Mel laughed and replied, "Have your coffee and take a bath, my sweet, and then we'll go down to breakfast and see if there are any other guests still hanging about. While you're doing that I'll read the papers."

When her husband emerged, still towelling his hair and looking for his change of clothes, Melpomene said, "Nothing here about our case yet – but this is interesting, Alex, I see that there is a big scandal looming at the Foreign Office – '*An ambassador from one of the Caribbean countries has accused an official of the British embassy in his home country of major currency offences involving close to a million Pounds Sterling. Arrests are expected, but the police in that country and here are being very close-lipped'* – I wonder what that's all about?"

She read on, "Oh, wait a moment, here is something that will appeal to you, *'The European Lawyers' Amateur Golf Championship will this year be held at the Enfield course, starting next Wednesday and running until Sunday. The vice-captain of the club, Dr Roger Ransome, said that they were gratified to have received entries from all over Britain and from such countries as France, Denmark and Germany. The competition will be confined to the front nine holes, so that ordinary members and their guests may still enjoy playing, as well as spectating.'* I suppose that means that you will be heading there on Wednesday, will it, Alex? Excuse me if I don't accompany you, my love, you are well aware of my attitude to the game! So that leaves me free to follow up Phoebe's enquiry – I'm afraid you will have to go by train to Enfield, as I shall need the car."

"No problem, Mel, I used to go by train when I was at University – there's a good service and the course is an easy walk from the station, even carrying a set of clubs."

They went down to the dining-room, where the usual Castle Hotel breakfast was waiting in a series of *bains maries.* Melpomene constructed herself a huge plate of eggs, sausages, bacon, fried tomatoes and fried bread, while Alex limited his selection to scrambled eggs, toast and marmalade. They both had Lapsang Souchong tea.

There was only a sprinkling of other guests there, but Melpomene's Mama, Lady Cynthia Musgrave, and her Aunt Isabel were chatting with their old friend, Superintendent David Wilkinson, of the Hampshire Constabulary. As Mel and Alex passed them, the two ladies and David all greeted them warmly, Lady Cynthia remarking, "We were all saying how successful it was yesterday – did you two enjoy it as well?" which brought a warm acknowledgement from the pair.

When they had almost finished the meal, Alex started to ask what they should do for the rest of the day, saying, "I suppose we should aim to set off back around six-ish – we don't want to have another late night!" And then Phoebe appeared at the door, peered around, and, spotting them, came and sat down next to Melpomene.

"Would you like some breakfast?" Mel asked, but Phoebe declined with thanks, "I had my usual porridge, and I'm full up! If you don't mind, I rode here on my bike and brought a whole lot of stuff for you!"

She put a stack of papers on the table, and proceeded to go through them. "This is Janice's name and home address, when she's there, which isn't often. They have only a small permanent staff, and extra people come in when the parents are in residence. At the moment her mother and father are in Saint Luke, which is an island not far from Jamaica. It's a former French possession, she told me, but has been independent for ten years or so. I suppose they could be reached at the British Embassy there – I think Janice's father, Colonel Lionel Sharpe, is the military attaché, whatever that is!"

Phoebe went on, "And this is the prospectus for our school, Hillyard House, which is near Brighton, up on the South Downs. It is a boarding school, mainly, but there are a few day girls who live in the neighbourhood – only half a dozen, I think. As well as the prospectus, I brought the Student Handbook, which has all the rules and regulations in it. The headmistress is an Anglican nun, Sister Angela Boniface – we call her 'Bunnyface' when nobody's listening. She's generally quite nice, but tends to be strict with us. None of the other teachers are nuns, but there is a chaplain, who is also the curate of the local church. We don't have much to do with him, but we have to go to chapel on Sundays, of course."

"Very good!" said Melpomene, "Of course we know your mother and father quite well, and I suppose Janice's parents are on good terms with them, too, since she often comes to your place in the holidays, is that so?"

"Yes, and they often telephone each other when she is here, so Mummy and Daddy would know their number in St. Luke. Could you not bother them too much with all this, though, unless it is really necessary – I don't think Janice would like it, and Mummy, especially, can get worried very easily."

"Trust me, Phoebe!" said Mel, "If I need to speak to them I will check with you first. Is there anything else you want us to know now? If you think of anything later, you can always telephone us at home or at the office. You know all our numbers, I think."

Phoebe gave Mel a hug and a kiss, and shook Alex' hand, "Thanks ever so much for offering to do all this!" she said.

Chapter 2

Mel and Alex spent the rest of the morning quite lazily, reading the papers and, in Mel's case, doing the Times crossword, but after lunch they decided to go for a walk. It was a little too cold for tennis, and in any case, the green-keeper was top-dressing the courts ready for the winter, so they put on their boots, wrapped themselves up well, and set out to walk along the many paths in the woodlands surrounding the hotel grounds, taking Monty, the hotel's resident beagle, along with them.

There were great heaps of fallen leaves that had collected under the trees and by the edges of the paths, and Monty was very busy searching out interesting scents and snuffling through the leaves. He occasionally gave an excited yap as he startled a rabbit, but he had been trained not to chase them, and then, when Mel and Alex were at the point of turning for home, he found something more interesting, half buried by leaves. Alex poked at it with his stick and discovered that it was a bundle wrapped in sacking. He was inclined just to leave it there, but Melpomene's curiosity had been aroused, so Alex tore the sacking off, finding that it was pretty rotten and came away easily, revealing a leather briefcase, quite mouldy but securely locked.

"We should take it back to the hotel and try to open it there!" said Mel, "There could be small items inside, and we don't want to lose anything in the leaves!"

So, once they were back in their suite, Alex picked the briefcase lock, which was very cheap and elementary, and turned out the contents onto a sheet of newspaper. There was a wizened blackish object that could have once been an apple, two or three pencils, a ring with three Yale-type keys, while the rest were all papers, some in folders, others in envelopes.

He passed the envelopes to Melpomene, while he attended to the loose papers and the folders. Mel concentrated on the addresses first, which seemed mostly to be 'Mr and Mrs A. Ogilvie, 4 The Limes, Woodhampton', 'A. Ogilvie, Esq,' or 'The Occupant', finding that many of those addressed by name seemed to be personal letters, such as thanks for hospitality, while the 'Occupant' ones were advertisements or the like. Then she found one, to 'Mrs Olivia Ogilvie', that made her whistle, and she read it out, "Listen to this, Alex, what do you make of it? *'Dear Mrs Ogilvie, I am surprised that you have not seen fit to respond to my previous letter. I should stress again that I regard the matter as extremely serious, and point out that inaction on your part can only lead to outcomes that you will sincerely regret! I would recommend that you consult your legal or financial adviser without delay. I shall expect a reply within the week or I shall be forced to take drastic action. Yours faithfully, Arthur Greenslade.'* There is no return address, neither on the letter nor the envelope. If it were not for the bit about 'consulting your legal adviser' it would sound rather like a blackmail demand – what do you think, Alex?"

"Hang on, Mel – perhaps you are looking for drama where none exists – it's just a strongly-worded demand for payment of some kind, that's all – blackmailers rarely sign their demands!" said Alex.

There was silence for a while, punctuated only by more murmurs like, "boring!" or "rubbish!" from Mel as she looked at each letter, and then Alex sat back with an interested expression on his face.

"Was the signature on your 'blackmail' letter 'Arthur Greenslade', Mel? If so, I've found what it's all about. This folder has all the correspondence from him, with carbons of Mrs Ogilvie's replies, and the main item is – wait for it, Mel, this is serious – a hire-purchase agreement made between Olivia Noreen Ogilvie and Arthur Greenslade, trading as 'Greenslade Cycles', for the purchase over a twelve-month period of a Raleigh child's tricycle, for a total of £2/19/6 or twelve instalments of six shillings and sixpence! This is high finance, Melpomene – it appears that the poor lady had dropped behind in her payments! All this for a matter of a few bob! And have you noticed the dates on those letters?"

"I see what you mean, Alex – they are all dated at least four years ago. This briefcase has been lying in the woods for years, which explains its mouldy condition! Let's go down for afternoon tea now, I'm getting quite peckish!"

"Oh, yes, Mel – it must be close to three hours since you had any sustenance! Off we go!"

Afternoon tea was being served in the garden room, and they found several people had had the same idea, including Melpomene's Aunt Isabel, so they asked if they could join her at her table. "How's life, Auntie?", asked Melpomene, "Stephen Buckmaster was complaining that he never has any interesting cases brought before his Magistrate's Court – is it the same with the Children's Court? Oops! I'm sorry, you are not supposed to discuss details, are you?"

"That is correct, Melpomene, but there is no harm in relating one or two interesting accounts, as long as I mention no names or other details that might identify people, especially the children. I'll give you an example from about four years ago – in any case it made the newspapers then, so there is no longer any need to be completely confidential. A young child, aged about five or six, was brought before us by the police, charged as a person being in need of care and attention. It transpired that the child's father had disappeared and the mother had been thrown into such a state of despair that she took her own life, having sent the child next door to play with the neighbours' children, which she did quite often, apparently."

Melpomene spoke up, "Excuse me for interrupting, Aunt Isabel – what do you mean by 'charged as in need of care' or whatever you said – do they actually charge the victim in these cases? This sounds inhuman to me!"

"You misunderstand a little, Mel – there is no implication that the child is to blame – this is simply a way of ensuring that proper proceedings are taken," explained Aunt Isabel, "in this case especially, who else was to be charged? Anyway, I'll continue my story. We, on the bench, that is Stephen Buckmaster, Annabelle Higgins, matron of the cottage hospital and myself, determined that the child be placed in the care of her maternal grandmother, and, as far as I know, there she still is, when not at school – I'll tell you about that later. Other agencies have taken over the responsibility for oversight now, and the police have set in train their procedures for tracking down the missing father, in case he could be found and made to renew his parental responsibilities – I do not know whether they have yet been successful. If you want to look all this up in the newspaper files, the name of the missing father is Anthony Ogilvie. There was a lot of interest at the time, there are a number of articles in the respectable press, as well as in the tabloids, speculating that he murdered his wife, but the Coroner had no doubt that she gassed herself – there were no indications of violence, either on her body or in the house."

Chapter 3

Melpomene looked as though she was about to comment on what they had found out about the husband, but Alex put his fingers to his lips and shook his head. "You mentioned the school that the child is attending, Lady Isabel," he said, "what were you going to tell us about that?"

"It happens that Stephen Buckmaster is on the Board of Governors of Hillyard House School, where Phoebe goes, and he is also the trustee of their scholarship fund, so he nominated this unfortunate child for a scholarship, and since than she has been attending the school – and doing very well, Stephen tells me!"

Mel and Alex told Aunt Isabel that it was very interesting hearing these things, and that they hoped she and Stephen would continue to have fascinating cases in the Children's Court. They made no mention of their discovery of the briefcase, and later agreed together that they would not discuss it until they had a clearer idea of the possible implications. They said they would probably not see Isabel at dinner, as they would have to get Marjorie and Winnie back to London in good time, so they bade her farewell, with kisses and hand-shakes.

Melpomene was very pleased to have found out that Stephen Buckmaster was a Governor of Hillyard House, saying, "This might make it easier for us to get to talk to Janice – we shall have to think very carefully about all this! And I'm afraid that, as a detective, I have the scent of this Anthony Ogilvy in my nostrils! As soon as we get back to London – or at least, tomorrow – I shall quiz Jimmy about the police missing-persons records and see if we can do any good with hunting him down."

"You're assuming he has gone to ground?" asked Alex, "I, on the other hand, wonder whether he is still with us on Earth or has been bumped off. We don't know enough about him to decide which is more likely – it would be too much of a coincidence to find out that he has anything to do with Janice's worries!"

"Let's have another good look through the briefcase, Alex. We might see something that we passed over before, now we know a bit more of the story. And maybe we should have a hunt round the place where Monty found it – if we give him his head, he might sniff out something else. We should get out there while it is still light! But, at a pinch, we could come back another day – if the briefcase has been there for some years, another few days won't make any difference. But let's have a quick look now, or I shan't get any sleep tonight!"

They soon found the place where Monty had found the brief-case, but no matter how much he snuffled and scraped around that area, nothing turned up, so they shrugged their shoulders and went back to the hotel to round up Marjorie and Winnie.

They found that they had been playing ping-pong in the new games room, "We had to play in bare feet, because we had only brought boots and high heels with us, no plimsolls – but it was great fun!", said Winnie, "I used to play ping-pong regularly, and badminton, too, at the Regent Street Polytechnic sports club – Maureen introduced me as a member – so maybe you would be interested in taking it up again, Marjorie – you're really quite good!"

Said Melpomene, "I might even be persuaded to join you both – I used to use the facilities there when I was a student at LSE, and now that the tennis season seems to be over for the year, I am in need of some healthy exercise. Alex has his golf – I don't believe that that is really exercise, but he won't listen to me!"

"We'd better all go up and pack to go home," said Alex, "if we're too late this evening, Marjorie's Mum will start to worry. And we'd better telephone Mrs M to check whether she is intending to cook dinner – if not, we'll go to our Italian place."

Two hours later, they were taking their seats after being welcomed by Guiseppe at his trattoria near Liverpool Street Station, as usual prepared to take pot luck – he had never failed them! They were soon sharing a huge dish of *pollo alla cacciatora con funghi,* following it up with a selection of *gelati.* Even Melpomene pushed her chair back at the end of the meal with a sigh of satisfaction!

The girls were dropped off at their homes and Mel and Alex arrived back at the flat to find that Caroline, the house-maid, and Mrs Mountain, the cook-housekeeper, had already turned in. So Mel made cups of chocolate, and the two bathed and went to bed, dropping off almost as soon as their heads hit the pillows.

The next day they both woke early, ready to start the working week with a new case – or possibly two, as Alex speculated. Their first move after breakfast was to ring Jimmy Manley at Mile End Road police station. Detective-Constable Cec Thompson, Jimmy's right-hand man answered the telephone, saying, "I'll get Jimmy to ring you back – he's in with the Super at the moment. Did you have a good celebration? As you know, I was unable to come, as someone had to stay and mind the CI department – and, as it happened something did turn up, that's what Jimmy is discussing with the Superintendent now – no doubt he'll fill you in when he calls back."

"We're off to the office now, Cec," said Alex, "so he should allow us enough time to get there before he calls."

At the office of 'Crabbe and Crabbe, Private Investigators' Marjorie and Winnie were rearranging the furniture yet again, so that either of them could as easily get up and answer the doorbell.

"We shall have to have another go at this, once we have the new filing cabinets and so on," said Marjorie, "but it is already working quite well. No calls so far, and the postman hasn't been yet."

"Jimmy Manley will be ringing soon," said Melpomene, "it sounds as though he might have something new for us."

"As long as it doesn't stop me going off to Enfield for the golf!" said Alex, "If I don't have a break now, it will be Christmas before we know it!"

They were soon all drinking their first cups of tea of the day and eating jam tarts. Marjorie had explained to Winnie the importance of getting in their regular supply each morning, "I really think that without jam tarts, Melpomene in particular would soon wind down like a clockwork mouse!"

And then the telephone rang, and Mel answered it, while Alex picked up the second ear-piece.

"Jimmy here, Mel, I hope you are all recovered from your excesses of the weekend! We have a new investigation coming up here, and I think it sounds as though we might want to call on the services of a reliable detective agency. It concerns something of a diplomatic nature, so it could be politically sensitive. If you like, I'll come over and fill you in with the details. Are you willing to give a hand?"

Chapter 4

Jimmy Manley arrived at the office within the hour.

"Cup of tea, Jimmy?" asked Mel, "We've got decent brands as well as what they serve in your canteen!"

"Now, now, Mel! You know that Cec and I brew our own, so you don't have to sneer. Earl Grey, please, if you run to it! Have you wolfed all the jam tarts yet?"

He sat down with them in the back office, which now boasted a conference table and some decent chairs.

"As I said on the telephone, this is a sensitive one, so what I tell you mustn't leave this room. My super had a visit last Friday from a locally-employed officer of an embassy not far from our patch – as you may know, there are embassies scattered all over London – I'll give you the full details if you decide to take on the case. This official, who claimed to be at a fairly high level in the hierarchy, but not in the confidence of the Ambassador, told Superintendent Watkins that he had approached the police here because he suspected that there was some sort of conspiracy under way. He didn't know who was involved, so he was reluctant to confide in his immediate superior, nor anyone else in house for that matter."

"What sort of conspiracy?" asked Alex, "Espionage, illegal immigration, drug running, arms smuggling, or what?"

"Either one or more of those, or common or garden embezzlement or theft, he thought. What he was basing his suspicions on were sudden displays of affluence by colleagues paid no better than himself – ranging from new suits or designer dresses up to flash cars, or in one case, a new villa at Southend-on-Sea! He couldn't work out how they were doing this, as finances are scrupulously checked by the embassy comptroller. He himself had been made to answer some searching questions about lunches he had arranged for legitimate visitors to the embassy."

"So, Jimmy," said Melpomene, "how do you propose to go about this enquiry? It can't be a simple matter to get into any embassy – unless you are applying for a visa or something – and their records must be strictly looked after. My first idea would be to start with these people that Mr X suspects, and work back from there. Do most of the staff live locally?"

"You're right, Mel, I agree that would be a good approach to try first. As for where they live, the Ambassador and his family and aides occupy a residence that is part of the main embassy, which has been converted from a row of terrace houses in a Regency square, so the family is guarded in the same way as the rest of the establishment, very securely indeed. But other staff, whether locally-recruited or from the home country, live out, either in officially-rented houses close to the embassy, or in flats and houses like any member of the general public."

"What about servants, Jimmy?" asked Mel, "I suppose they are vetted meticulously too, otherwise I could try to get a job as a housemaid or somebody!"

"No chance, Mel! Hiring is checked by the same Home Office department that validates household staff for Buckingham Palace – in any case you haven't got the skills to be a good housemaid! Perhaps a junior scullery maid, but they would only take kids for that!"

"Come on, you two!" said Alex, "You are getting off the point with these flights of fancy! We need practical ways for getting good information on staff activities, inside or outside the embassy itself."

"So it really seems that you intend to undertake this investigation!" said Jimmy, "Which means that I ought to put you properly in the picture – can we have another cup of tea first? And, since Marjorie and Winnie will inevitably need to be involved, they should join us before I lay it all out."

Marjorie made a new pot of tea, and Winnie reported that she had seen that the jam tart supply was getting low, so had popped down to Mrs Jenkins' and bought a fruit cake and some doughnuts. So they were all busy for a few moments, until Jimmy rapped with his teaspoon on his cup to catch their attention.

"The embassy concerned is that of St Luke, an island republic in the Caribbean, a former French colony, now independent."

At this, Melpomene and Alex looked hard at each other. Jimmy, noticing this, asked, "Have you had something to do with that country before?"

15

"Not yet, Jimmy," said Mel, "but maybe in the future. We'll tell you more later!"

Jimmy went on. "The St Luke's embassy occupies nearly the whole North side of Yeominster Square, near Hyde Park, and it has permanent leases over several other dwellings in that square, as I have found out from my contact at the Foreign Office. There is a clearly-marked main entrance about half-way along, where those offices which deal with the public, such as the visa office, are located. I cruised past there recently to get a feel of the set-up, but I haven't been inside."

Jimmy took another sip of tea and continued, "My informant came in person to Mile End Road, explaining that he did not want to use any police station nearer to the embassy, for fear of being spotted, as he didn't want to have to invent a reason for seeing the police. The embassy has its own branch telephone exchange, so he couldn't call from there either. His name is Walter Huskisson, third secretary of the commercial division, dealing with commerce between St Luke and Britain – he covers agricultural products, chiefly bananas and sugar."

"Now we come to the nub of the matter! He has strong suspicions that one or more of his colleagues are using diplomatic bags to run arms or drugs between here and St Luke. Apparently piracy in the Caribbean did not end with the demise of Blackbeard and Henry Morgan – and rum-running has seen a big surge since prohibition began in the United States in 1920."

Melpomene was puzzled, "But you wouldn't get many guns or much alcohol in a diplomatic bag, would you?"

"The term doesn't just apply to something like a briefcase, Mel," explained Alex, "It refers to any container that can be sealed, even one big enough for a motorcar! There are international conventions that prohibit third parties from opening or interfering with items that are marked accordingly. However, as you might assume, for the most part, a diplomatic bag would contain documents of a confidential or secret nature."

"So, if I were bent on smuggling something," said Mel, "I could just get my colleague, the responsible officer, to seal and mark the box or whatever as a 'diplomatic bag' and it would get to its destination untouched! And the profits from the transaction could be returned the same way!"

Chapter 5

Alex suddenly remembered that he had seen an article in one of the Sunday papers about currency offences concerning a Caribbean country, but he couldn't recall the circumstances, "I don't think they mentioned the country – could it have been St Luke, I wonder? Maybe they've picked up the story in today's papers. Marjorie, you're good at this, can you do a bit of a search for us, please?"

While she was looking, the others carried on with the discussion, Melpomene saying, "If you would like us to take on this case, Jimmy, we ought to start by speaking to Mr Huskisson – should we go to him, or will he come to us, in the first instance?"

Jimmy said, "I will give him the names of you two and your agency – he is going to bring me some documents this afternoon, so I'll put it to him then. I think he ought to be given the choice of consulting you, or just keeping it a police matter."

Marjorie came back into the room waving a copy of The Trumpet, "Found it! Let me read it to you. *'SERIOUS ACCUSATIONS BY THE ST LUKE AMBASSADOR: London, Sunday. At a press conference at the St Luke Embassy in Yeominster Square, His Excellency the Ambassador, Chev. Dominique de Chapelle, stated that he had incontrovertible evidence that an unnamed officer of the British Embassy in Port Sylvestre, the capital of St Luke, had illegally transferred an amount in local currency equivalent to nearly a million pounds sterling to a bank in the Bahamas, said to be favoured by international gangs for financing the traffic of small-arms to the Americas from eastern European countries. He went on to say that the Foreign Office and the Metropolitan Police had been informed.'* There's more, but that covers the main points. That paper tends to be a bit sensational, so I'll look through the straight-laced ones too."

"You said that you two had had something else to do with St. Luke, Mel," said Jimmy, "do you want to tell me about it now?"

"Yes, but I don't think it has any connection with your Mr Huskisson," said Melpomene, "it is about a school-friend of Phoebe Buckmaster, Stephen's daughter – you met her at the hotel on Saturday – nice girl, very bright. Phoebe has become rather worried about her, because she is in a very depressed state and won't talk about it. Anyway, her father is a diplomat at the British Embassy in St Luke, that's the only connection so far as we know. Phoebe has asked us to try to find out what is upsetting the child. We shall have to be careful not to be indiscreet – there are already rumours spreading at the school and we don't want to make them worse – schoolgirls in their teenage years in the hothouse of a boarding school are likely to blow any small whisper up into a major drama – believe me, I've been through it all myself!"

"Quite a coincidence, all the same!" said Jimmy, "But don't let us emulate your schoolgirls and make too much of it! As I said, I am going to see Huskisson this afternoon – I'll call you and let you know what transpired. Thanks for the tea and doughnuts, and I'll get Cec Thompson onto following up that story about the St Luke ambassador. Since His Excellency stated that the police and the foreign office had been informed, it is now an open matter for us and doesn't belong exclusively to Huskisson. See you all later!"

After Jimmy had left, Marjorie found another relevant story in a more respectable newspaper, but apart from using different language, the only extra piece of information was that the Ambassador had ordered a thorough check of the bank accounts of all the London staff, regardless of status and seniority, to be conducted by a reputable firm of auditors in the City. He added that this was likely to take at least six months to complete.

"And now he has warned all those who are on the fiddle to cover their tracks immediately!" remarked Alex, "I suspect that this is an exercise in whitewashing, not detection!"

"If he had wanted to seek out the villains, he should have come to us, or to someone like us!" said Melpomene, "Perhaps we should ring him up and suggest it!"

"One step at a time, Mel dear – lets wait and see whether Mr Huskisson approaches us first. And I have just recalled something – I must be getting forgetful in my old age – about the case that Aunt Isabel related to us. She said that the missing father was being looked for by the police – I wonder if he was ever found?"

"We could ask David Wilkinson to find out for us, Alex – I'll try telephoning him now – Marjorie, have you got Superintendent

Wilkinson's number at Woodhampton? If so, I'll talk to him and Alex can listen."

In a few moments, David Wilkinson was on the line, and Mel was greeting him warmly, "Hello, David, Melpomene here! It was a good party on Saturday, wasn't it – I saw your wife enjoying playing cards with some other ladies in the evening, while you were chortling in a corner, swapping reminiscences with a bunch of your old friends over whisky-and-sodas or something! What I rang about is shop, I'm afraid. My Aunt Isabel was telling me that there was a case in the Children's Court about four years ago, involving a suicide, in which the unfortunate woman's husband, a Mr Anthony Ogilvie, disappeared and was being sought by the police. Is it at all possible to follow this up, David, and let us know whether he was ever found? If so, this might help us in an investigation we are pursuing for someone else. I can't tell you much more at the moment."

"I vaguely remember the case, Melpomene – there was a little girl involved, too, wasn't there? I'll certainly chase this up for you. How's business? Caught any fresh murderers lately? Your Mr Banfield will be up at the Old Bailey soon – I'm told that a Harley Street psychiatrist is going to give evidence that he is off with the fairies, so he'll probably finish up in Broadmoor rather than on the end of a rope! This is all off the record, of course! By the way, I'm quite impressed with your staff – I had talked with Marjorie on the phone a lot from time to time, but she seems even brighter in person, and the other one, Winnie, is a clever girl, too!"

"They're staying with us, David! But you'll probably see them personally from time to time – Winnie has already shown she is capable of working independently – she did some good work in Northampton, helping to track down some more of the art mob. Well, nice seeing you at the weekend and talking to you now, David, keep in touch!"

"Certainly Mel – and I guess Alex has been listening, too. I'll let you know what I find out about Anthony Ogilvie, if anything. And my regards to Jimmy Manley, I guess you are still working hand-in-glove with him!"

When he rang off, Alex said, "We must remember to maintain cordial relations with Northampton and Huddersfield, too. Our work is going to rely more and more on these networks!"

Chapter 6

Alex asked the secretaries if they had brought anything for their lunches. Marjorie said that her Mum always sent her off with something nice, while Winnie said she was going to pop out later. He said, "We're going out to get a pie or something for ourselves, should we bring you anything, Winnie?"

"Oh, yes, Alex, that would be nice, maybe a pork pie and a couple of tomatoes, please."

Mel chose a couple of croissants, a piece of blue cheese and a bottle of ginger beer, while Alex had crisp rolls and some ham.

As they were finishing and turning to drinking cups of tea, the telephone rang, and it was Jimmy, who told Melpomene that he had Mr Huskisson still with him, who was wondering whether it would be convenient if he called at the office very soon – Jimmy had told him which Underground station to head for and where the office was to be found.

It was no more than half an hour later when the doorbell rang and Winnie showed Huskisson in and introduced him to Melpomene and Alex. He was, to everyone's surprise, very short in stature, with a close-cropped grizzled beard, and maybe fifty years old. He stepped forward and wrung the hands of Alex and Melpomene, who led him into the back office, asking whether he would like tea or coffee.

"I don't touch either, thank you," he said, in a rather high-pitched voice, "could I perhaps have just a glass of water? I'm afraid I have very definite ideas about diet and health – some of my colleagues call me a crank, especially when they find out that my wife and I are vegetarians – but not extremists!"

This confession caused Alex to hesitate, but Melpomene was not at all perturbed, led him to a chair and said, "Detective-Inspector Manley has told us a very little about your quandary, Mr Huskisson – perhaps you wouldn't mind starting at the beginning for us, would that be alright?"

"Certainly, Mrs Crabbe, we must be meticulous in these matters of course. It started very gradually, when I was surprised to see some of my colleagues, at grades both higher and lower than my own, making purchases that I judged were not congruent with what I judged their salaries would normally permit. I cannot say for certain when the first such realization dawned upon me, but it must have been at least nine months ago – it was certainly at a time when the weather was inclement, because what I noticed was that a colleague who occupied a desk adjacent to mine had suddenly become blessed with a magnificent pair of Russian leather boots of a striking burgundy hue. I admitted to him that I had noticed them, and he vouchsafed the intelligence that he had, only a day or two earlier, purchased them from a famed boot-maker in St James's Street. To my embarrassment he then went on to boast about the price he had paid for them – close to my salary for half a year."

Mr Huskisson paused at this point, sipped his water and dabbed his forehead, which was beginning to glisten. He went on to list a number of similarly surprising acquisitions that he had noticed since, being careful to point out that he had not since allowed himself to make comment about them. There were more instances of both men's and women's footwear, expensively tailored woollen suits and designer dresses, even, as Jimmy had mentioned, a new villa at the fashionable end of Southend-on-Sea.

Melpomene asked him, "How general was this rash of affluence, Mr Huskisson – did it involve most of the embassy staff?"

"Oh no!" he said, looking scandalised, "I should have made it clear to you at first that it involved only two or perhaps three of my male acquaintances, and, I think, one lady – although it is sometimes difficult for me to make judgments about ladies' dresses and coats. I worried for a long time whether I should bring my suspicions to the notice of anyone in authority at the embassy, but hesitated in the absence of any conclusive evidence of improper conduct. And then, as you will have realised, I decided to seek the help of the detective branch of the police force."

Said Mel, "You were certainly fortunate to have approached Detective-Inspector Manley, we have worked with him several times and he is very resourceful, thorough and intelligent!"

"And, may I say," said Huskisson, "that he regards your agency with similar respect! Might I point out at this stage, that the use of discretion is paramount here – but I'm sure that you understand this well! Can you give me any idea of how you propose to tackle this task?"

"Certainly, Mr Huskisson," said Alex, "first, we can assure you that we have a similar attitude to privacy that you would find in a family solicitor – I am, as it happens, a solicitor myself. Next, we need to be guided by your knowledge of the workings of your embassy and of the diplomatic service as whole. A question to begin with – have you any colleagues inside or outside the embassy who you would be prepared to take into your confidence to any extent? What I have in mind is not complete disclosure – merely someone you could ask to do small tasks, like getting hold of documents that you yourself have no access to? How are documents managed in general – are there filing cabinets open to all and those to which the keys are kept by certain officers? Is there any system which keeps account of who has what documents to work on at any time, or is this left to individual discretion? Do you keep any documents yourself, or is it all managed centrally? A lot of questions, I'm afraid!"

"My word, Mr Crabbe!" said Huskisson, "You sound as though you have worked in an embassy yourself! I will describe our systems to you in detail later, but in response to your first question, I do have someone in mind who we might call upon for assistance – on a limited number of occasions, you must understand – I was at Edinburgh university with him and have known him for thirty years or more. He is second-in-command in the Comptroller's office."

"Very good, Mr Huskisson – by the way, could we use first names so as not to be so formal? I am Alex, and my wife answers to the name Melpomene, or sometimes just Mel! I have not worked in an embassy, but legal firms are quite careful with document control!"

"Then you may call me Walter – not Wally, if you please! I have brought some papers with me for your perusal – please keep them secure, and I shall need them back in no more than two days. If you wish to copy any of the contents, please do not include the identifying headings or the names cited therein. This one might be of most interest, it is the comptroller's annual report detailing totals expended in a number of categories, including salary details. You will see that my own emolument is far from lavish and could not run to too many new suits, and certainly not to hand-made boots!"

Chapter 7

"Would you like anything to eat, now, Walter?" asked Melpomene, "We can offer you apples or oranges – we ourselves normally snack on such items as jam tarts and fruit-cake, but do I assume that these are not acceptable to you as a vegetarian?"

"Quite right, Melpomene, since most pastries and cakes contain butter and sometimes eggs, both of which are anathema to my wife and I. On the other hand, we will eat water-biscuits or Scottish oat-cakes, but I don't suppose you count these among your staples here."

"Let me just ask Marjorie."

The resourceful Marjorie discovered a packet of Matzos, still unopened, which she had bought for a Jewish client before finding that she was non-observant and would happily eat anything. Walter Huskisson gratefully accepted one of these, an apple, and another glass of water, and continued his account.

"It was my old friend who passed me the comptroller's report – it is not intended for general circulation, but mainly for the information of those we might regard as the 'cabinet' within the embassy, comprising His Excellency the ambassador himself, the head of chancery, the comptroller, the chief of protocol, the military attaché and the press attaché. These officers are not all of equal rank, but owe their membership of this inner circle to their function. To explain the detailed administration of the whole embassy I think is unnecessary for our purposes – and I'm not altogether sure that I understand it completely myself! As a humble third secretary, I am not required to do more than oversee trade agreements and occasionally to intervene in matters of dispute over contracts."

"You mentioned the press attaché, Walter," said Melpomene, "Would I be right in suspecting that such a gentleman would keep his ear to the ground, monitoring rumours as well as facts?"

"You are right, except that in the St Luke chancery this person is not a gentleman but a lady! Her name is Elizabeth O'Connor – she had a long and distinguished career as a foreign correspondent for a major daily newspaper, and has built up an extensive network of contacts in several arenas, in addition to the diplomatic and political ones. I believe she has but a year or two to run before she retires."

"Would I be jumping to conclusions," asked Alex, "if I hazarded the guess that she is one of those who you have recently observed making unusual expenditures?"

"You are right!" said Walter, "But I hope that your remark depends in no wise upon the gender of this person, but rather on her occupation!"

"Of course, Walter! I have long since been cured by my dear wife and partner of any lingering disparaging attitudes towards the sex! So, we have identified one of the apparently dishonest company – was her extravagance of a major nature?"

"No, relatively minor, Alex, though noticeable withal! A sudden tendency toward the wearing of very fashionable dresses at official and social functions, whereas, as my own dear wife remarked, her wardrobe was formerly rather on the dowdy side! That reminds me, I don't quite know why – our silver wedding is coming up in a few days, and I have been given the task of finding a suitable restaurant where we might entertain a few friends and workmates, including that lady. Perhaps you could recommend an establishment – as long as it offers some vegetarian dishes."

Melpomene piped up, "Walter, would you and your wife be able to accept Alex and me as friends, too, after such a short time? If so, it might afford us an opportunity to see and talk with some of your colleagues. We will certainly have no trouble in picking you out a suitable restaurant, we have been frequenting this general area since our university days!"

Alex took up the suggestion, "You need not, of course, disclose that we are detectives – Mel is in fact a social anthropologist by training, and quite capable of relating many illustrative anecdotes dealing with that field, while I am a genuine solicitor in good standing with the Law Society!"

"This is beginning to sound like a very pleasant idea!" said Walter, "I shall put it to my wife as soon as I get home today – we have been talking only in general terms about a suitable way of commemorating our twenty-five years, but I would imagine that a nice dinner out would be greeted with enthusiasm by Marie-Colette – did I mention that my wife is French?"

Melpomene continued, "I should very much like to meet her, Walter, and I'm thinking that it would be nice if you would invite the two of us to your home – this will enable us to get acquainted, and to make it easier for Alex and I to behave like your old friends when we go to the restaurant. Your other guests may then relax enough so that we can subtly lead them into disclosing useful information about any of their irregular practices."

Walter Huskisson was looking happier and more confident now, and said, "Whether or not anything useful emerges over dinner, it will establish your roles as social acquaintances as you say. I have your telephone number, of course, so I will talk to Marie-Colette this evening about inviting you round to our house – would tomorrow be too soon? Our anniversary is in two days. Our address is 12 Yeominster Square – next to the the chancery building, and I'll give Marjorie my telephone numbers, at work and at home."

Once their visitor had gone, Alex said, "As usual, my darling, you have come up with a bright suggestion at the right time! When we talk to the Huskissons tomorrow, we must lay more ground-work, so that they will be able to respond appropriately if we seem to be overstepping the bounds of polite chit-chat at the restaurant."

"I rather hope," answered Melpomene, "that the guests have sufficient wine at dinner to loosen their tongues! I imagine that as well as being vegetarians, Walter and Marie Colette are likely to be abstainers – but we shall have to wait and see! It could either be a productive evening or no more than a social occasion. Have you thought about a suitable venue? Walter will probably have to book a table, depending on the number of guests he has in mind."

"Do you remember, Mel, that nice French place where we celebrated setting up Crabbe and Crabbe? That's in Mayfair, not too far from Yeominster Square – as long as it's not too expensive for the Huskissons!"

"Oh, come on, Alex – you've seen Walter's salary – they are not paupers, they just can't afford hand-made boots! Anyway, if he jibs, we can think again!"

Chapter 8

Just as they were preparing to leave the office that afternoon, Walter Huskisson rang to say that his wife would be delighted to entertain Melpomene and Alex for dinner the next day, in their home, at half past eight, no need to dress, saying, "Marie-Colette was very pleased with the prospect – she told me in no uncertain terms that it was about time we widened our circle – some of the people at the embassy are pleasant enough, she said, but she said of others, 'ils sont vraiment barbants!' – she mentioned no names!"

Alex said, "We ought to let Jimmy know what's happening, I'll telephone him now." He reported to Mel that Jimmy was happy about it, but had warned them not to get too enthusiastic at the restaurant, saying "If your dinner companions' tongues can be loosened by a glass too many of wine, the same could happen to you, you know!" Alex assured him that they were well aware of such dangers, had become accomplished at deception as a staple of their profession and in any case would imbibe in moderation!

After breakfast the next morning, Melpomene said, "I know we don't need to dress for tonight's domestic dinner, Alex, but the restaurant is a different matter – I think I would like to treat myself to a new frock! I suppose your dinner jacket is still reasonably clean – if not there is a drycleaners nearby that will do a sponge-and-press in an hour. I don't suppose you wish to accompany me on a trip to Bond Street, do you?"

"No, no, my pet, but if you are willing, you could drop my dinner suit off for me on the way to the Tube. I shall go to the office – you don't want the car do you?"

"Right oh, then, Alex! I'll probably come to the office, too, after I have succeeded in my quest – I have no idea what I shall be looking for yet! See you later!"

When Alex arrived at the office, Winnie had obviously been waiting for him, and said, "Oh, Alex, could you please telephone Stephen Buckmaster right away – he sounds a bit nervous, so I'll get him for you. He's not in court this morning, he says."

"Hello, Stephen," Alex said, once he had settled down with the telephone, "what can I do for you? Winnie said it sounded urgent."

"Well, I don't honestly know whether it is or not!" replied Stephen, "I've just been speaking to Phoebe at her school. She wanted to ring you or Mel, but the Headmistress at Hillyard House has decided to enforce her rule about girls only being allowed to call their parents. They have to place calls through the school switchboard, which has a list of permitted numbers for each of the girls. Sister Boniface, the Headmistress, is obsessed with preventing them talking to boys, I suppose! At least she has the decency not to listen in!"

"This sounds very mysterious, Stephen, but I think I might have an idea what it is about. I don't know how much she has told you, but she has asked Melpomene and me to find out why her school-friend Janice has become withdrawn. Since we have been back from Woodhampton, I'm afraid we have been so busy we've done nothing about this."

"That makes sense, Alex – she said she hadn't wanted to bother me or especially her mother about it – Eugenie tends to work herself up about anything to do with the children, so I can understand Phoebe's reluctance to confide in us too much. Well, to get to the point, Phoebe wanted to tell you and Mel that Janice has run away from school! The teacher who goes round every morning, to wake the girls up and make sure they wash and so on, found that her bed hadn't been slept in and there was a pillow in it to make it look occupied. Miss Templeton knew that Phoebe and Janice are chums, so she asked Phoebe if she knew anything – but she didn't, and so got very upset and tried to ring you – and had to be content with me instead! So I took it upon myself to take emergency action, spoke to Sister Boniface and said that I would come and collect Phoebe after lunch. The headmistress said they all had tests in the morning, which they shouldn't miss – but how Phoebe is supposed to concentrate, I don't quite know. Anyway, I shall drive to the school in an hour to pick her up, but I wanted to talk to you first!"

"And what is the school doing about the missing Janice?" asked Alex, "Have they contacted the police, or what?"

"Yes, they have, and while I was talking to Sister Boniface, she said that the local Sergeant had turned up and was taking statements from everyone in sight! I suppose we'll find out more when I pick Phoebe up this afternoon."

Alex went on, "I gather that Janice sometimes stays with her grandmother in the holidays, unless her parents are in the country, but grandmother lives in Scotland, so she can hardly have gone there. Phoebe told us that there are no boys involved, as far as she knows. It's quite a puzzle! So, Stephen, please let me know if anything happens, or if you find out any more from Phoebe. I shall be here in the office all day – Melpomene is out shopping."

Alex busied himself with a few routine matters, like signing cheques for the household and office bills that Marjorie had been looking after. While he was attending to these, the office doorbell rang and Winnie took delivery of a couple of cartons which turned out to be the new office stationery, complete with the headings that they had all agreed to, and envelopes with the return address on the back.

"We are beginning to look like a proper business!" he said to the girls "Uniforms for you two next!" Winnie and Marjorie both laughed at this.

The telephone rang once more and it was Stephen Buckmaster again.

"I had just set out for Hillyard House, when who did I see getting off the bus but Janice Sharpe! She was on her way to our place. At first, I thought of taking her with me to the school, but fortunately, before I mentioned it, I realised that this might make Janice suspect I was taking her back to school, so instead, I took her to our home and gave her into the care of Eugenie. I shall set out again in a moment, but I thought I should let you know that she appears safe and well, and even a bit cheerful! More later, once I get Phoebe home!"

"That sounds very promising!" said Alex, "With both girls there, you might find out some more."

"Oh, no!" protested Stephen, "Phoebe has engaged Crabbe and Crabbe for this task, and the last thing I want is to be coming the heavy parent! Besides, you and Mel have the requisite skills for what could turn out to be a very tricky and sensitive undertaking. I will even restrain myself from pumping Phoebe on the trip home! I'll get her to phone you and Melpomene once we're back!"

Chapter 9

Melpomene arrived back at the office at about three o'clock, carrying not one but two large boxes bearing the name of a famous Bond Street store. Marjorie and Winnie clustered round her expectantly, while Alex pretended not to be particularly interested.

Unwrapping layers of tissue paper from the contents of the first box, Mel held up a dazzling confection of a dress, a long and straight gown in plissé satin of a rich golden colour, with a sheer beaded overdress.

"I won't model it for you now – I merely point out that this is not intended for our dinner party tomorrow, but for the next grand ball we attend! I'll fold it back into the box carefully soon, but meanwhile I'll show you the other, which I shall wear tomorrow evening. It is nice, I think, but not dramatic – we want to talk about matters other than fashion!"

The dress was indeed more restrained, but nevertheless up to the minute, in a dark green velvet, which Melpomene acknowledged was her favourite fabric, quite low cut, especially at the back, but not as long as the ball gown.

Marjorie and Winnie were praising both dresses fulsomely, when the telephone rang and Alex picked it up, "It's Phoebe, Mel, do you want to pick up the other earpiece?"

Phoebe said, "Oh, Alex – such a lot has been happening today, but I'll start by saying that Janice seems to have become a lot calmer than before, which is very encouraging to me. She'll speak to Melpomene on her own in a moment, as she wants to talk about rather personal matters. But I can tell you that she got up at about two o'clock last night, got dressed in the girls' bathroom, in her warm overcoat, scarf and gloves – no hat, because our school hats are instantly recognisable – and slipped out through the French windows onto the terrace. She first walked to the local railway station, which only took her twenty minutes or so, but found it in darkness. When she looked at the timetable outside the ticket office, she found that the first train in the morning would be a London train, stopping only at Brighton and two more places, so she decided not to wait but to walk into Brighton, which she knew would take about an hour – we've done it in a crocodile with our whole class before now.

I'll hand over to Janice now, if you can pass the telephone to Melpomene, please, Alex."

Janice started rather shyly, "Hello, Mrs Crabbe – we have met before, at Phoebe's house. She tells me that she has spoken about me to you and your husband and that you have both kindly agreed to help me – which makes me rather conscience-stricken and bashful. It seems a bit much to take up your time over the silliness of a schoolgirl!"

At this point, Mel said, "No need to be apologetic, Janice, Phoebe told us a few days ago that you were in a very depressed and worried state, so we are only too glad to do what we can to help! Please go on, and tell us everything that might be relevant, however trivial or petty it might seem to you."

"Thank you very much – I'll try to do it without sounding like a baby! I've tried talking to the teachers, and even to Sister Boniface, but they just said I should pull my socks up and not worry – or things like that! If there was a single person behind all this, it might be easier, but when it's just a matter of little jibes from a number of girls, it's hard to make anyone see why I'm getting so upset! How it started was when one of the prefects said words like – 'you think you're something special, Sharpe, because your father is a diplomat – but diplomats can be dishonest, too, you know!' And when I tried to defend him she just said that of course I would take his side."

Janice broke off, and Mel could hear that she was getting worked up, breathing in a series of sobs, almost, so she said, "Take it slowly, Janice my dear, I'm listening, and I don't think you are being silly! Call me Melpomene, and go on, please, were there any other accusations like that?"

"Oh yes, Melpomene, I began to think that there was some sort of ganging-up going on – after a while there were only one or two girls, like Phoebe and Amanda, another close friend, who treated me properly. Everyone else either ignored me or made nasty little remarks that I could hardly hear as they passed by, like 'here comes Her Excellency!' or 'be careful, girls, count your pocket-money!' After a while I started hiding when I could, in between classes and meals and so on. And when these spiteful ones saw I was upset and crying, they nudged each other and made remarks about that, too! How can people be so cruel! And then somebody found an article in one of the Sunday newspapers saying that an ambassador from a

Caribbean island had accused an official in his home country of stealing or something as bad! You can imagine what these girls made of that! So I thought that I had to get out!"

"I can quite see how you were feeling, Janice – go on if it doesn't upset you too much."

"No, its good to get this all off my chest, Melpomene – I haven't been able to talk about it much – I didn't want to burden Phoebe and Amanda with it or get them into trouble. I knew I would need some money, so I went to Miss Hardwick, the Bursar, who manages our money for us – we get a weekly allowance of pocket-money for the tuck-shop and for any small items we need – and I spun her a yarn about wanting to buy my mother a birthday present when we were next in Brighton – we get taken there in groups some weekends to visit the museum and things like that. And she let me have most of my account – several pounds. And last night I made my escape, as you know!"

"I tell you what, Janice," said Melpomene, "We have engagements today and tomorrow, but after that, Alex and I will motor down to Woodhampton Castle Hotel, and you can come and we can have a big discussion about what to do next. Have you tried to telephone your parents in St Luke at any stage since this all started happening?"

"No, because Daddy has always stressed that his work is important and that I should telephone him only for real emergencies – and I was worried that he would pooh-pooh all of this just like the teachers!"

"So we'll talk about this, too – you realise that the school will have to contact your parents about you running away, don't you? Phoebe has told us that Sister Boniface called the police in as soon as you were found to be missing, so they would get in touch with your parents even if the school hasn't done so already. That's not the sort of thing that can be overlooked! I should think that as soon as your parents hear about it they will try to reach Major Buckmaster and his wife – they know you often go to their place in the holidays, so it's an obvious place to try! And your grandmother, too, I should think. Anyway, we'll have to try sorting it all out when we come down. Would you ask Major or Mrs Buckmaster if I could have a word with one or both of them, please, Janice, and, meanwhile, try to relax with Phoebe – you know she is a true friend, don't you?"

Chapter 10

Stephen Buckmaster came on the telephone, "I'll tell you first of all, Mel, that when I collected Phoebe from school yesterday I told Sister Boniface that Janice was safe and well and at our place. She said that she had tried before to telephone Colonel Sharpe at the British Embassy in St. Luke, but that because of the time difference they were not answering, so now she knew Janice was safe she would not trouble him, saying 'He gets rather testy with people he sees as interrupting his work – I suppose he is an important and busy man after all!' I got the feeling that the Sharpes were not among her favourite parents!"

Mel said, "Please tell Janice about that very soon, Stephen – she is worried that her father will overreact, I think. He does give the impression of being rather a martinet! Go on, Stephen, please."

"The headmistress also said she would call off the police, which is good, but there might be some point in getting David Wilkinson to contact his Sussex colleagues to find out whether the policemen who came to the school had kept notes of what they were told there. A good detective might be able to pick up some clues from these! As I told you, I had no intention of questioning Phoebe in the car on our way home, but she was full of it all, of course, and chattered about nothing else. She said that there was a particular clique – Susan Saxby was one girl whose name was mentioned – who 'had it in' for Janice and were going out of their way to be spiteful to her. I don't know how long ago this all started – when Janice was with us over the summer holidays she seemed quite carefree – you saw her briefly then. It certainly wasn't that Sunday newspaper article that triggered it off – that merely added fuel to the flames."

"Thanks, Stephen, I'll talk to you further when we are in Woodhampton in a couple of days. As I told Janice, Alex and I will come to the hotel then, and we can all have long discussions to plan the next phase of our investigation. We have recently made some contacts in London which might be helpful as well – I can't say any more at the moment. Meanwhile, I recommend ping-pong as a suitable means for getting the girls' minds off the subject – tell them to remember to take their plimsolls. Our Marjorie and Winnie played it at the hotel last weekend and had a great time! I'll catch up with you later!"

Melpomene put the telephone down with a sigh, "Adolescent girls! I'm glad I was never one myself! I'm expiring for want of a cup of tea, – can you oblige, please, Winnie or Marjorie, and tell me – are there any goodies left?"

"Don't fill yourself up too much, Mel!" said Alex, "Remember we're going to the Huskissons' this evening! Not that a vegetarian meal sounds as though it would be very filling – but to be fair, I'm only guessing, I've never actually had such a meal."

"Oh, yes you have!" replied Melpomene, "Don't you remember that nice Lebanese restaurant on the Rive Gauche that time? We had mezze and avoided the meat skewers. Oh I do hope the Huskisson's cook has heard of baba ghanoush, tabouleh and kibbeh! My mouth is starting to water at the thought!"

"Anyway, we ought to get home, Mel – I guess you'll need to carefully select what you will be wearing this evening, won't you? I shall just change my shirt and go in the suit I have on, if you think that's all right."

"And I'll have to do my hair properly, Alex, we need to create a good impression with Mrs Huskisson, since she is used to entertaining diplomats!"

They drew up outside the Huskisson abode, fashionably ten minutes late and were admitted by a maid, who took them to a sitting-room where they found their hosts waiting.

Melpomene had been careful not to make too many assumptions about Madame Huskisson, but any that she had made would not, as she said to Alex later, have come anywhere near reality. In sharp contrast to her husband's commonplace appearance and manner, Marie-Colette was a ravishing blonde, who must have been a full twenty years younger than Walter, and was dressed as though she had just been photographed for one of the society illustrated magazines. She came forward and embraced Mel, kissing her on both cheeks in the continental manner, and then seized Alex' hand between hers and kissed him, too.

"I will make it my business to uncover your entire *histoires, tous les deux*, before I venture to bore you with that of Walter and myself. Would you like a glass of something before we go in?"

On offer was fruit juice and sparkling mineral water, Mel and Alex both chose the latter – Marie-Colette was already drinking orange juice. Just then the maid entered again and ushered in a young man, who came up to Marie-Colette and was kissed on both cheeks by her. She then introduced him as Philip Seaward, and explained she had invited him that evening for two reasons – first because he was without a partner, as he was *'entre deux aventures amoureuses'* and might feel uncomfortable in the mixed gathering at the restaurant – and secondly because he was not attached to the embassy formally, but was often called upon to audit their accounts as an independent expert and hence might be useful in any investigations that the Crabbes might want to pursue.

"I am expecting no-one else," announced Marie-Colette, "so let us take our places in the dining-room. You may bring your glasses."

The same maid who they had seen before brought in the first course – celery soup – and Walter explained that they had only a modest staff, a cook-housekeeper and Bridget, the maid. "People of higher rank are provided with servants by the embassy, and so are we, when we are called upon to entertain important guests – last week we had the Trade Commissioner and his retinue from an African colony here – but I'm afraid that you three don't qualify!"

Melpomene was delighted and Alex was relieved to find that they were served various Lebanese dishes as well as excellent salads, followed by an assortment of fruits.

As Marie-Colette had warned, she asked many questions, including the inevitable "Walter tells me you are an anthropological sociologist, Melpomene, so what, pray, is that?"

"He got it almost right, but not quite, Marie-Colette – actually I graduated from the London School of Economics as a Social Anthropologist!" and she went on to explain what that work entailed.

"And I know what a solicitor does, Alex – you deal with conveyancing of real estate, and with commercial contracts and wills and divorces, *n'est-ce pas*?" Alex was tempted to clarify her views, but decided that it would be unnecessary, even impolite, given the circumstances.

The conversation and meal enjoyed, Mel and Alex said farewell and that they looked forward to the next evening.

Chapter 11

The next morning, before she left for the office, Melpomene told Alex she would telephone Superintendent David Wilkinson to see whether he could find out what information, if any, had been gathered by the Brighton police when the girls and staff at Hillyard House were interviewed about Janice's departure.

"As for me, I'm off to my golf!" said Alex, "I shall be back at the flat in plenty of time to get ready for our excursion to the restaurant, so don't panic! I'll drop you at the office on the way, if you like."

Mel thanked him and said, "By the way, I've made an appointment to have my hair done later this morning – I wouldn't like my coiffure to let my dress down!"

At the office, Mel's call was answered by Inspector Wright who said that the Superintendent was out of the station for a while, but that he would ask him to ring back when he could. Mel took the opportunity to enquire which station of the Sussex Constabulary was closest to the school, and Wright said he would find that out before he spoke to David Wilkinson.

Just then, Winnie came in, bearing a box from Mrs Jenkins' shop, "Jam tarts anyone?" she called, "And I got a few mince pies, too – Mrs J said she was starting to get ready for the Christmas season – all the shops get earlier and earlier every year, even though it's still weeks away! Alex not in today? – well all the more for us, then!"

After cups of tea and a discreet selection of pastries, Marjorie said that she would put the rest somewhere out of sight, "Otherwise we shall all spoil our slender flapper figures and have to buy new skirts and jumpers!"

David Wikinson rang, unknowingly breaking up the playful dispute which threatened to ensue among the girls, and telling Mel, "I got onto the police at Brighton East station – they are the ones who cover the area of the school – and the station sergeant said that the two men who had covered the incident had quite full descriptions of their interviews in their pocket note-books, and had just finished copying the main points into the station day-book. He fetched it and read it out, and he will send a copy – I told him not to send it to me, but to Jimmy Manley at Mile

End Road, as you were in frequent touch with him. He should have it by tomorrow or the next day. There was one entry that I found particularly interesting – shall I read it to you, Mel?"

"Oh, yes please, David, hang on and I'll get Marjorie to listen on the other ear-piece and she can write it down in shorthand, too. Right-oh, go ahead, David."

"Here we go: Recorded by PC Ollenshaw, date, time, etc, etc. *'Interview with Miss Susan Elizabeth Saxby, aged 16, boarder, Hillyard House School, who claims that Miss Sharpe must have run away because she knew her father was about to be arrested. On further questioning, Miss Saxby said that she knew this because her own father is an important official in the Foreign Office and had told this to Miss Saxby's mother in her hearing'.* How about that, Mel? This girl sounds as though she has formed a strong opinion one way or another! Whether there is any truth there we have yet to discover!"

"Thanks very much, David. Janice already identified this girl as a member, even the leader, of a hostile clique at the school! When we get the full transcript via Jimmy, we'll be able to see if there's anything else of interest!"

She rang off and sang out to Marjorie and Winnie, "Off to the hairdressers' now, ladies! Have a good look at me now, you might not recognize me when next we meet! I shall go straight home afterwards, so that I'll have plenty of time to get pretty for tonight!"

While she was waiting for her hair to dry, Melpomene leafed through the magazines provided, finding with great interest in the most recent copy of Vogue that her new ball dress was right up to the minute. They also had one or two daily newspapers of the sensational kind, so Mel looked to see whether there was anything of interest to do with the firm's current investigations, but drew a blank there. Then she noticed that the lady under the next hairdryer was reading a copy of 'The Tatler', but as she glanced over, the woman threw it down in exasperation and exclaimed, "It's only the nouveau riche these days who catch the eyes of these journalists!", then spotting Mel's amused gaze, said, "I must apologize for my outburst, my dear, but I get quite annoyed sometimes! I was interviewed at length myself, only a week or so ago, and was promised a paragraph in 'About Town', but they've filled the column up with nobodies! I should introduce myself, now that I have disturbed your tranquility! I'm Lady Diana Widdicombe, can I know your name, dear?"

"Well, since we're disclosing titles, I'm the Honourable Melpomene Crabbe, née Musgrave – you may know my Mama, Lady Musgrave, of Woodhampton Castle."

"You wouldn't believe it to look at me, but I was actually at school with Cynthia, your mother – she was a prefect while I was a little mouse in first form! Please remember me to her next time you are at home – I was Diana Forbes-Blenkinsop then, but I don't suppose she'll recall me from schooldays, we were too far apart – but we have bumped heads a couple of times since!"

Just then the hairdresser came to take Mel from the dryer and embark on the cutting and styling, so she waved to her new acquaintance and went into the main salon.

Back at the flat, Caroline helped her get her dress ready for the evening, but she wasn't ready to put it on yet, so while she was waiting for Alex to arrive back from the golf course she did a couple of crossword puzzles. Then she remembered her encounter at the hairdresser's and telephoned her mother.

"Does the name Diana Forbes-Blenkinsop mean anything to you, Mama? She says she is Lady Diana Widdicombe now, but that she went to your school, several years behind you."

"How did you meet this woman, Melpomene? I would strongly advise you to have as little as possible to do with her – she is a confidence trickster! Yes, it is true that she is married to Lord Widdicombe, all right, but he is in the same game and has spent time in prison for it, too. I have found all this out through David Wilkinson, who tells me that they work fashionable events, like Ascot, or Henley Regatta, convincing the innocent that they have inside information and will lay bets for them – of course the horse or crew that they pick always comes in well down the order, and they invariably have an excuse – the horse was nobbled, or the crew were ill – whatever they think of at the time. They never actually put any bets on, of course, just pocket the stake money. What sent Roy Widdicombe to jail was that he let slip the name of the horse he was supposed to be backing and it went on to win. Unluckily for him, the punter he was trying to swindle was an off-duty police inspector! Since his unfortunate holiday as the guest of His Majesty, neither of them discloses the name of whoever or whatever they are supposed to be backing!"

Chapter 12

Somewhat to Melpomene's relief, Alex kept to his undertaking to arrive back in plenty of time to get ready for the restaurant, so she asked him how his golf went.

"I didn't expect to win any trophies, but I didn't think I was as out of practice as all that. I went round in 64, which doesn't sound so bad until you are told it was for nine holes!"

Mel made suitable commiserating noises and said that maybe she should encourage him to practice more, despite her well-known antipathy to the game.

While they were both making their final touches to their preparations, they had a discussion about what they had learned the previous evening.

Mel said, "I was at first rather dubious about getting anything worthwhile apart from the plain facts from Walter – he seemed rather a stick-in-the-mud civil-service type – but having met and talked with Marie-Colette, I have revised my opinion somewhat. She certainly has some life about her, wouldn't you say? And he must have more going on beneath the surface or she wouldn't regard him as positively as she obviously does."

"The expression 'attraction of opposites' came to my mind, Mel, they exhibit it to a much more extreme degree than is the case with you and I, my darling! We would not, of course, make such an effective partnership were we to think and react the same way about everything! What is your opinion of the accountant, Philip Seaward? Should we take him into our confidence?"

Melpomene pondered a little, "I would like to find out more of Walter's and Marie-Colette's feelings about him before we commit ourselves, Alex. And we'll see tonight who else we have to deal with, of course. There's probably going to be a lot of rivalry going on among the guests, with any luck – it could be an excuse for people to let their guard down, especially after a few glasses of wine! You might get a chance to do a bit of minor flirting, Alex, me too – all in the cause of professional investigation, of course!"

They arrived at the restaurant in good time and, leaving their coats and scarves in the cloakroom, approached the *maître d'*, telling him they were with the Huskisson party, *"Ah, oui, Madame et Monsieur,* we have put you in our private dining room, as your party is of substantial size. Please walk this way."

Walter and Marie-Colette were waiting just inside, and greeted Mel and Alex warmly, with the customary kisses and hand-shakes, and then took them to a couple standing sipping champagne. Walter said, "I'd like you to meet Anthea and Ben Waterman – Ben is my second-in-command in commerce, and Anthea is a writer of novels – of some repute, I believe – you will have to catechize her sternly, she is not one to shout about it!"

Marie-Colette then said, proud at getting it right, "Alex is a solicitor and Melpomene is a social anthropologist – if you want to know what that is, she will tell you, I'm sure! Now let us go to our places, I think that there are only one or two still to come. Mel and Alex, I have put you one on each side of me, so I can tell you quietly what I know about everyone! And Walter will sit on your other side, Alex, so that he can do the same!"

There was a choice of celery soup or a clear consommé, Marie-Colette announcing, "Each course will have at least one vegetarian selection – those who are uncertain can ask me which is which!"

When people had been served their choice and had their wine-glasses filled, Walter turned to Alex and said, "Now I will start to tell you about them all! And my dear wife will do the same for Mel, I'm sure. For a start, I told you the other day about our press attaché, Elizabeth O'Connor – she is that distinguished-looking lady on the left, near the end of the table. As you see, her white hair is elaborately coiffed, and her dress comes from the latest collection of Worth or Balenciaga – I am no expert, for details you should ask Marie-Colette or the lady herself. Next to her, the gentleman in the tuxedo, who appears to be hanging on her every word in between spoonsful of soup, is my old university friend from the comptroller's office, his name is Desmond McPhail – you can trust him, I believe."

Walter mentioned several more names and gave his prima facie opinions of them, until he indicated a couple who were apparently having a minor dispute, under their breaths.

"They are Brigadier and Mrs Cedric Douglas – he is of the same embassy rank as myself, and his ostensible role is Military

Attaché, which you may know is frequently a diplomatic euphemism for spy. I'm not completely sure, but I have a feeling that Leonie, his wife, suffers from some long-term medical condition that often leaves her exhausted. She seems fairly fit at the moment."

After the main course, which, to Melpomene's approval, offered several Lebanese delicacies as well as chicken and roast beef and a variety of salads, Marie-Colette stood and said, "Ladies and gentlemen! Before the sweet course arrives, I give you all my permission to change places, or indeed to leave the table altogether. I am told that the sweet dishes are already served as individual portions, so you may take a plate and a fork and wander about as you wish. This is an extra benefit of being in a private dining room!"

When there was a general move to comply with that suggestion, Melpomene seized a beautifully-presented banana-split boat and headed for the Douglases. As she reached the couple, Mrs Douglas excused herself, saying that she didn't feel up to standing too long, and went to settle down on a settee at the back of the room with a fruit cocktail. Mel asked Douglas if he wished to look after her, but he demurred, saying, "Please don't concern yourself – I'll keep a general eye on her – this is usual for Leonie and it doesn't distress her. For myself, I would like to know what a social anthropologist does, I hear that is your profession, is it not?"

Melpomene explained in general terms – she was well practiced in this – and then said, "I am equally puzzled about the functions and duties of a military attaché – is it really true that they include espionage?"

Brigadier Douglas laughed at this, but Mel could see that she had touched a nerve, and he said, "No, no, Mrs Crabbe, my work is to do with liaison with the British armed forces, like arranging guards of honour for State visits by St Luke notables, and organising training programs for their Army – which, I might say is no more of a threat to any other country than the Boy Scouts! The closest I come to your implication of espionage is that it is my job to monitor newspapers and broadcasts for any mention of threats from other countries or activist groups, either to this embassy or to St Luke itself."

"Are there any such threats at present?" asked Melpomene mischievously. "Not at all – none that I could reveal, anyway!"

Chapter 13

Melpomene pursued her questioning further, "You say that the role of a military attaché is largely liaison with the armed forces of the host country – does this extend to the civil security forces, such as the police, coastguards or customs services?"

Douglas sat up a little straighter and narrowed his eyes, saying, "Do I detect a special interest here, Melpomene? Perhaps you have studied the sociology of such organizations – I imagine that bodies who have a vested interest in security, or even in clandestine operations, would exhibit particular characteristics, would they not? To take this notion further, one could say that the very nature of our diplomatic service is founded on the careful manipulation and control of information, am I right?"

Melpomene was thinking very fast – it would be very tempting to be drawn into such a fascinating discussion, but this man was revealing himself to be unexpectedly perceptive, and she would have to be extremely careful – no, better play it dumb!

She laughed lightly and said, "Were I writing a doctoral thesis I might well engage you in some such deep discussion, but I am not – I merely have a residual interest in such matters, which is not worth following up, especially on a social occasion such as this, which we must remember is to celebrate Marie-Colette and Walter's silver wedding anniversary. Is someone going to make a speech, do you know?"

While Mel had been engaging Douglas in conversation, Alex had been doing the same with Elizabeth O'Connor, the press attaché. After introducing himself, he asked her how she got into the field of diplomacy, saying, "I'm told you had a very successful career as a journalist and foreign correspondent – did that get too exciting for you?"

She gave a brief laugh, "By implication, you believe that diplomacy is dull and boring? I can assure you, that is far from the case – let me relate to you a case that I have been dealing with lately." She paused to take a sip from her glass of red wine, not the first of the evening, as Alex judged from her high colour and wandering gaze.

"This all started with an article in a recent Sunday paper, which, I must confess, was based on what I had leaked to an acquaintance of mine on that publication – it is one of the functions of a press attaché, I believe, to provide a supply of stories to the press. Unfortunately, in this case, I had overlooked the potential of that item to build into a scandal, and I had to work very hard to rein my friend in – not entirely successfully, I fear. What I had originally seen as a throw-away comment on the temptations that might be offered diplomats, with a hypothetical example provided, turned into an overt accusation of wrong-doing by an officer of the British Embassy in St Luke. I'm beginning to think, regretfully, that the time is approaching when I must retire – I cannot risk further slips of this sort!"

Alex saw his chance to pump the lady further, while she was still in an indiscreet mood, "But surely, Elizabeth – if I may call you that – no names were mentioned, were they?"

"Of course not! I may have been careless, but I would not reveal identities! I referred, in my hypothetical example, to 'an official of a British Embassy, working, say, in a Caribbean country, who might be offered a monetary inducement by a local to reveal details of trade negotiations' that's all! The trouble is that in the Caribbean area, a large proportion of the countries are British colonies, which have High Commissions, not Embassies, so he seized upon St Luke! And, since my employer is the Ambassador of that country, he put two and two together and made five! The 'million pounds sterling currency offence' was pure invention – the paper must have been short of news that weekend! I need not assure you that this was the last leak that that periodical will get from me!"

"I suppose you tackled them over this – will they publish a retraction?"

"Oh, yes! But the paper comes out weekly, and the coming issue has probably already gone to bed, so by the time the retraction is published it will all be far too late! And nobody reads retractions, anyway, they usually bury them on an inside page!"

"So, now, Elizabeth," said Alex, "may I take this opportunity to pick your brains a little? You must realise that I am a complete ignoramus – as far as the processes of diplomacy go, at any rate – so, tell me something. If you, as a member of this St Luke's Embassy, wanted to find out about some questionable practices at the British Embassy in St Luke itself, how might you go about it? Who would you approach first?"

"You might think," said Elizabeth, "that the obvious course would be for me to speak to my opposite number, the press attaché there – but this takes no account of the fact that we as a breed are very jealous of the information we possess – it is our only coinage! No, instead I would most likely approach someone in our comptroller's domain and ask him or her to speak to the comptroller in St Luke – unlike press attachés, they usually trust one another! I have actually done this once or twice over the last couple of years – I am on good terms with Desmond McPhail and was just talking with him at the table during soup – you might find it worth your while to talk to him if you really want to follow up this line of enquiry."

"That is very interesting, Elizabeth, but I had better leave it for now – I see that Walter is rising to his feet, so I believe he might be getting ready to thank his wife for twenty-five years of wedded bliss!"

That was indeed the case, as Alex spoke, Walter clinked his fruit salad coupe with a spoon and made an announcement.

"Ladies and gentlemen," he said, "thank you all for coming and making our little celebration into something really special. I shall call for toasts to the bride very soon, but before that, I have my own duty to perform. Marie-Colette, please come here and accept this gift as an inadequate token of my gratitude for putting up with me for a quarter of a century."

Marie-Colette actually blushed and went and embraced her husband, who handed her a small box wrapped in silvery paper, which she opened, disclosing a pendant watch, cased in silver. She placed it round her neck and then went round so that all could admire it, saying to Walter, "*Merci tellement mon chéri*, I don't think I deserve one as expensive as this – it is from Patek Phillipe, everyone!"

Then she stopped and said, "Lest you all think that my darling Walter has missed out, I have a watch for him too!" and she opened her reticule and produced a gold wristwatch, which she buckled on to his wrist, while she announced, "It is a Cartier, and I chose it because it is French, as I am myself!"

Everyone flocked round, and then they all toasted the happy couple before they made preparations to leave.

Chapter 14

On the way home in the taxi – they had both decided that they had imbibed a little too much to drive safely – Alex said, "You know, I believe Elizabeth O'Connor was spinning me a line about her part in the Sunday newspaper story – even the most irresponsible journalist would hesitate to mention an Ambassador unless he had been given evidence of his involvement, and Elizabeth said she had simply advanced a hypothetical case. I have never believed the saying '*in vino veritas*' – most of the time it's quite the opposite. Anyway, we know that Walter suspects her of being one of those involved in shady dealings."

Mel agreed, "She was wearing a gown which must have cost over 300 guineas – way out of the reach of even a successful private investigator, let alone a humble press attaché!"

The next day, Melpomene and Alex drew up in their Riley tourer in front of the porte-cochère of the Woodhampton Castle Hotel just in time to join everybody at lunch. Mel's Mama and her Aunt Isabel were there, so there was a lot of kissing and hugging, and Mel had to give a full account of all that had happened in the past few days. Then she asked Lady Cynthia, "Are Phoebe and her friend Janice around, Mama – we came down specially to talk to them – have you seen them this morning?"

"I should try the games room, if I were you, dear – they have organized a ping-pong tournament for the children of the staff, which has been going since early morning – they arrived here on their bicycles even before I had finished breakfast! What a nice pair of girls they are!"

A general hubbub was audible before Mel and Alex entered the games room. There were two tables in play, and Phoebe and Janice were just finishing a game – which Janice won, by two points. Their table was soon taken by a pair of determined-looking ten-year-old boys, so the girls came up to Mel and Alex, Phoebe saying, "Shall we go somewhere a bit quieter?" and leading the way to a sitting room at the other end of that floor.

Melpomene gave both the girls a hug, and sat next to Janice on a settee. Janice was bubbling over, wanting to say something, so Mel told her to go first.

"Mummy telephoned me at the Buckmasters' yesterday afternoon, Daddy was at work and she wanted to speak to me privately. Our headmistress, Sister Boniface, knowing that I was safe and well, wanted her to let me know that she understood what I had been going through, and said that there were to be no recriminations when I returned to school, which she hoped would be soon – she asked Mummy to point out that although she sometimes behaved like a harridan, she sympathised with the girls, knowing that a boarding school is a poor substitute for a home. Wasn't that nice of her? But Mummy had something else to tell me."

"What was that?" asked Mel, "Nothing too bad, I hope."

"Well, good and bad, I suppose! She said that Daddy had decided to end his tour of duty in St Luke and return to England to ask for another assignment. He needed to give a good reason for this, because diplomats are bound by rules and regulations like other public servants, so he is saying that it's because of Mummy's health – so she wanted to let me know that she is, in fact, perfectly healthy, before I read it in the papers. A press release is always issued in these cases, she said. What I'm a little bit anxious about is Daddy's real reason – he, as an ex-army officer, doesn't do things on a whim! And there's all this talk about illegal dealings!"

Melpomene said that was all very interesting and that Janice must be looking forward to seeing her parents again, for a while, at least. "And I have another piece of news for you, too," she said, "that article in the Sunday paper was a made-up work of fiction! Some over-enthusiastic reporter took a remark which was meant to be speculation and dressed it up out of his own imagination! I know, because I spoke yesterday to someone at the Embassy of St Luke who told me the whole story. No particular country was mentioned and no sum of money, either! The paper is going to publish a retraction in a forthcoming issue, but, as usual with these irresponsible actions, harm has already been done!"

Janice was obviously relieved, and said, "Thank you, Melpomene! I'm feeling a lot better now, anyway – but how much of this is because I'm away from those spiteful girls at school is hard to tell. I can't say I was looking forward to facing the music, and especially explaining myself to Sister Boniface, but now it will be a great deal easier. I was also reluctant to tell Mummy and Daddy, because it would upset them – and as well, I really didn't want them to take me away from school – I've only got a few years more and I'm doing quite well in my studies. If I get good results I stand a chance of getting a scholarship to a good University, I think."

Alex took over, "For my part, I've been exploring ways of getting inside information about the embassy, mainly so we can scotch any other rumours that might arise. Tell me, Janice, is it mainly the unpleasant comments about your father that have been causing you worry, or is there anything else?"

"No, Alex, not really. Of course, at any boarding school – or anywhere else, I suppose – there are always rivalries, silly squabbles and nasty remarks circulating among the little gangs that develop. I can cope with that – I'm used to it!"

Mel said, "I remember! I remember! But I have a further question, Janice. On the drive back from the school, Phoebe told her father there was a girl called Susan Saxby who seemed to be the ring-leader of one of the cliques. Later it turned out that she had told the police – who were called to the school by Sister Boniface before she knew you were safe with Major and Mrs Buckmaster – that she had learnt about your father's misdeeds by overhearing her own father, who she said was an important official in the Foreign Office, telling them to her mother. Did you know about this, Janice?"

To everyone's surprise, Janice burst out laughing, "If being in charge of the Foreign Office motor pool is important, yes he is. What Miss Susan Saxby doesn't remember is that a couple of years ago, when we were still friends, she showed me a photograph of him in a boiler-suit, when he was a foreman mechanic, before he was elevated to his present position!"

Everyone laughed at this. Alex then said, "If you can bring yourself to it, Janice, when you do go back to school – and I would advise you to do this sooner, rather than later – you should beard the Boniface in her den and explain that you ran away because things were getting so fraught. Maybe your mother could telephone her to offer some moral support. The headmistress has shown she has sympathetic feelings – even headmistresses can be human from time to time, you know – and very likely she will help you to settle back into your normal school life. And she might, also, read the riot act to those other girls for driving you to your extreme action of running away like that – as well as telling them not to copy you!"

Chapter 15

Phoebe said, "Janice and I have already spoken about this, and we are going to ask Daddy to drive us back to school this evening, or, better still, tomorrow, if he doesn't have to be on the bench then. Janice says she feels quite confident about talking to Bunnyface now, don't you, Janice?"

"Yes, I think this will help me to settle back into school routine," said Janice, "I have been too timid and retiring up to now, I've come to realize! As you suggest, I'll telephone Mummy in St Luke and ask her to tell Sister Boniface that she appreciates her offer to calm things down for me."

Alex asked, "Phoebe, are your parents at home now? If so, Mel and I might pop in and have a chat on the way back to London – we have other things we want to discuss with your father that haven't anything to do with Janice's escapade! You've got your bikes, I'm told, so you won't need a lift, will you?"

"No thanks – anyway, the ping-pong tournament isn't over yet!" said Janice, "The grand prize-winning ceremony happens at about four o'clock! We two are not contestants, but judges, of course!"

Melpomene rang the Buckmasters to make sure they would be welcome, then the two said farewell to Mel's Mama and Aunt Isabel, and set off for Woodhampton town. Eugenie greeted them at the door and invited them into the sitting-room with a series of questions, "Tea or coffee? – I assume you've already lunched? How did you find Janice? She seems to us to have become a lot happier than when she arrived the other day. How does she feel about going back to school?"

Melpomene replied, somewhat mischievously, "To take your questions in turn – tea, please – yes, thank you – we were told she was in the games room with Phoebe – we agree – she is quite reconciled, even looking forward to it."

Stephen came into the room then and greeted Mel and Alex, "Good to see you both! I take it you've talked to Phoebe and Janice? I'll drive them back to school this evening, but I'd better telephone first so they are ready for them – I would like to have a face-to-face chat with Sister Boniface, too – since she is a nun, albeit an Anglican, she might have some religious duties of a Sunday."

Then Alex said, "We'd like to have a chat with you, Stephen, about some unrelated matters, if you've got half an hour or so."

"I'll make myself scarce, then!" said Eugenie, "I'll get some tea and cakes brought in here – I'll say bye-bye before you leave for London."

"So, how can I help?" asked Stephen, "You said 'unrelated', so I take it that it's nothing to do with Janice, am I right?"

"Correct, Stephen, nothing to do with Janice directly – but it certainly concerns her father. I assume that you know that he intends to ask for a transfer away from St Luke – Melpomene and I are intrigued by this, because of rumours that have been circulating about his activities, implying that they might not be entirely above-board. As the saying has it, 'there's no smoke without fire'!"

"But you've convinced Janice that her father is innocent – I'm getting confused here!" said Stephen, "You'll have to explain it to me in words of one syllable, I'm afraid!"

"Indeed, I think Janice is no longer worried about the accusations that were made about her father, and I hope to keep it that way as long as possible. Melpomene and I made some useful contacts among embassy staff, and we intend to make discreet enquiries of them. But we also intend to investigate ways of getting information about Colonel Sharpe in other ways. We have no real idea what he has been up to, but it seems unlikely that he is leaving St Luke simply on a whim – there must be some more serious reason. There are several possibilities, but we're trying to keep an open mind."

Melpomene added, "Smuggling is one alternative – even gun-running among Caribbean nations, or rum-running into the States, seeing that Prohibition there has opened up many avenues for huge profits! We have contacts in HM Customs and Excise Service, so we'll make enquiries in that direction, too."

Alex went on, "We might even find that there have been *liaisons dangereuses* between the St Luke Embassy in London and the British Embassy in Port Sylvestre, which is where Colonel Sharpe is the military attaché. If diplomatic bags have been used in some sort of traffic between London and the island, there would need to be some sort of diplomatic representative at the Caribbean end. We shall see – or maybe this is just another dead end."

Stephen was very interested in all this, but finally asked, "But just where do I come in, if at all? Have I a specific role to play?"

"Certainly you have a role, Stephen," said Melpomene, "but anything but a specific one! Alex and I have become aware, on several occasions in the past, that any investigation inevitably generates a number of alternative solutions – these are, to an extent, vital to the process. However, if we allowed ourselves to consider every possibility, we should soon become bogged down. In our dealings with you, Stephen, we have come to see you as an ideal person to loosen up these traffic jams. We believe that your experience, first in the Army, and subsequently on the bench, has given you the facility to make prompt decisions that are neither hasty nor vague. So, we would like you to allow us to approach you whenever we get stuck! We promise not to overdo this – we don't wish to become a burden!"

"I'm happy to acquiesce, Mel and Alex! It will guarantee that I get to see the most interesting aspects of your work, while not needing to take any active part in your deliberations – apart from cutting the Gordian knot from time to time!"

They all celebrated this compact with a fresh pot of tea, accompanied by cucumber sandwiches and rock cakes!

Phoebe and Janice arrived back on their bikes in time to join in. "We had to split the grand ping-pong prize three ways," said Phoebe, "two girls and one boy all had the same number of winning games, and there was no time for play-offs!"

"What were the prizes?" asked Melpomene. "A ping-pong bat and a dozen balls each!" replied Phoebe, "Donated by your Mama, Mel – now they'll have to restock the games cupboard!"

The girls said goodbye and rushed off to get ready for the trip back to school, and Melpomene and Alex put on their coats and scarves for their return to London, after telephoning home to ask Mrs Mountain if she could provide a meal for them in an hour and a half.

Mrs M was happy to do so, as long as they would be satisfied with "Kate and Sydney pie follered by rhubarb 'n' custard", which they approved with alacrity!

Chapter 16

There were several telephone calls needing to be made, so Melpomene and Alex drove to the office straight after breakfast.

"The ping-pong was a great hit with Phoebe and Janice!" Mel told Marjorie and Winnie, "So much so that they organized a tournament for all the staff-members' kids at the hotel. It was appreciated by the staff parents as well – usually on a Sunday their offspring hang around the place being bored nuisances!"

"Now we need to make some telephone calls – what a blessing it is to have two lines now! First, I want to see whether Jimmy Manley is at Mile End Road station this morning – can you get him for me, please Marjorie? I don't know who Alex has in mind – if Winnie looks after his calls that should work out well."

Detective Inspector Jimmy Manley answered in his usual cheery way, "What can we do for you, Mel – do you want us to run in some villains this morning?"

"Not now, maybe in a day or two, Jimmy! First of all, did you get a report from the Brighton East police yet? They said that they were going to send you a copy of their day-book entries covering the enquiries they made at Hillyard House school when our young friend, Janice Sharpe, did a bunk from there. We've been told a little about it, but it would be good to see whether there are any other clues there that could be instructive. We have a lot of unanswered questions about the girl's father, who is a diplomat, so we will have to tread softly."

"I'll bring it over, Melpomene – in any case I would like an update on how you've got on with Walter Huskisson's case. And I have some extra information about that that you might find helpful. If I were to come over in an hour and a half, would that fit in with your programme this morning?"

"Excellent, Jimmy, we'll put the kettle on! See you soon."

Meanwhile, Alex had been talking to his contact in Customs and Excise, Senior Preventive Officer Ben Fisher, based at Tilbury Docks. He reported the conversation to the others.

"Ben Fisher was very glad to hear from us, especially when I told him what it was all about. I think he has rather a routine, boring life most of the time, dealing with small-fry criminals, as well as members of the general public who are simply trying it on with their liquor and tobacco allowances. As soon as I mentioned 'diplomatic bags', he seemed to perk up markedly. He told me that when such an item comes through his hands at Tilbury, the normal bond store goes into top gear. Anything of a diplomatic nature has to have extra lead seals attached – he proudly told me that he had been certified as a holder of a stock of seals and the special pliers that are used to attach them. Apparently the Embassy, Consulate or High Commission that is responsible for keeping track has one sort of seal, and HM Customs has another, and there are officials whose job it is to check each of them at each point in their journey. Ben said that there are also special 'tamper-proof labels as well, which indicate at a glance whether there has been any attempt to change the address or what have you on a package. So I asked whether I could go and talk to him about all this, and he was obviously quite keen! We'll arrange a time later."

"Jimmy is coming over soon, Alex – are there any other telephone calls we should make? Maybe we'll leave calling Walter until after Jimmy has told us what further information he has found out. Oh, I know – Stephen Buckmaster, to see how he got on with Sister Boniface. Marjorie – can you see whether Stephen is at home – we shouldn't disturb him if he's in court."

"There is someone else," said Alex, "Desmond McPhail, from the St Luke Embassy comptroller's office. Walter seems to think he is a trustworthy chap, and Elizabeth O'Connor pointed out that comptroller departments often talk to one another when financial matters are to be discussed. But if we're going to be talking to Walter Huskisson later, maybe we'd better check with him before we approach McPhail – we don't want to tread on others' toes."

Marjorie announced she had Stephen on the line, so Mel had a conversation with him and was assured that everything at Hillyard House seemed to be working out as desired.

"And there is something else!" he said, "Janice seems to have acquired a certain glamour as a result of her exploits! As I was leaving, she and Phoebe came to the car to say goodbye, and Janice whispered that a couple of the younger girls had come to talk to her with their eyes shining, and even the notorious Susan Saxby was making tentative overtures of friendship. Perhaps the headmistress had given her a pep-talk! And while I was there, I thought I would see how my protégée Lucy Ogilvie was getting on."

"Oh yes," said Melpomene, "Aunt Isabel told me how you had arranged a scholarship for her."

"That's right, and I was glad to be able to do so! So I approached Sister Boniface, this time in my capacity as a Governor, and asked her how the little girl was finding life at Hillyard House. She is eleven years old now, and in third year, and more than keeping up with the other girls in her class, so I was quite pleased. But then Sister Boniface said she had been meaning to bring something up with me and the other Governors. She had received two or three letters from a Mr Anthony Ogilvie, who claimed to be the child's father, wanting to come to the school and see his daughter. The headmistress immediately telephoned Mrs Edith Grantley, the grandmother with whom Lucy stays during holidays, to ask her about him. Mrs Grantley became angry and upset, saying 'He abandoned her, caused her dear mother to take her own life – and now he wants to take up with her again – have nothing to do with him, Sister! If I were you I would tell the police!' I asked Sister Boniface what, if anything, she had done, and she told me that she had thought that making enquiries with the police might risk stirring up the situation, which would not be in Lucy's best interests. So I asked her to leave it with me, assuring her that I would act with discretion. I took one of the letters away with me, but found that the address on them was false. Quite a mystery, Melpomene!"

"Oh yes, Stephen! You know, I'm inclined to follow this up – Alex and I have been wondering about Ogilvie ever since we found his briefcase in the woods. We surmised then that he had met his fate, somehow, but now we find he is alive and being a nuisance! If you don't mind, Stephen, I think that Alex might agree to Crabbe and Crabbe pursuing this mystery, if only for the sake of curiosity – an inescapable characteristic of those in the investigative professions!"

Stephen Buckmaster was all for this, saying that this allowed him to set it aside pro tem, so gave her his blessing, "Let me know if anything comes of it, please, meanwhile we'll let Lucy Ogilvie live in peace. Is it all right for me to tell Sister Boniface that it is being taken care of?"

Melpomene said of course it was – they would keep in touch.

Chapter 17

Jimmy Manley arrived just in time for 'elevenses' and immediately tucked into a jam tart and a cup of Lapsang Souchong, saying, "I was a bit slow to start appreciating this tea – it's very different – but I quite like it now. Here is the copy of the Sussex East day-book entries, Mel and Alex – I had a look through and found the Susan Saxby entry you had told me about, but there didn't seem to be much else of interest – to me, anyway! You have more background that I have, so you might have a different reaction."

"Thanks for that, Jimmy," said Mel, "we'll go through it in detail later. You would like to know what we have been doing with Mr Huskisson and everyone? Well, first of all we got ourselves invited to dinner at their house, where we met Mrs Huskisson, who turns out to be a glamorous Frenchwoman, much younger and livelier than Walter! We got on very well with her, indeed. She introduced us to a young man called Philip Seaward, who might be worth further cultivation – he works as an independent accountant, and is called upon by the comptroller at the embassy from time to time to audit their books. Marie-Colette – Madame Huskisson – gave us a lot more information about various members of the embassy staff which I think we will find very useful as we proceed with our enquiries. Then we contrived to be invited to a restaurant the next day to celebrate the silver wedding of Marie-Colette and Walter! Alex will tell you about that."

Alex took over the account, "Over dinner and afterwards, we both managed to have conversations with people who might turn out to be key players in this drama. I used my boyish charm to fascinate an elderly lady, Elizabeth O'Connor, the press attaché at the embassy. She is one of those suspected by Walter of splashing money around that might have been acquired in devious ways! She was certainly wearing an expensive-looking gown. But what interested me was that she admitted leaking a story to that rag, 'The Trumpet', which they amplified into a more-or-less direct accusation of malfeasance by a Caribbean diplomat – he was not identified, but everybody jumped to the conclusion he was someone at the British Embassy in St Luke, possibly Colonel Sharpe. This rumour gave his daughter, our young friend Janice, a lot of worry. Miss

O'Connor was evasive as she related her part in this, saying she just presented a hypothetical case – but I reckon she mentioned names, or at least dropped hints. We shall have more to do with her, I feel sure!"

"And while Alex was flirting with Elizabeth O'Connor," said Melpomene, "I was working my wiles on the military attaché at the St Luke Embassy, Brigadier Douglas – but I didn't get much from him, except the feeling that he is a very perspicacious operator and will need to be watched carefully! I started to ask him about his relationships with the police, Customs and Excise and the coastguards, but he was onto me in a flash, so I changed the subject – but he obviously does have such dealings, or it wouldn't have touched him like that!"

Alex nodded, "If he, as a military attaché, does get involved with those organizations, it is likely that his opposite number, Colonel Sharpe, has a similar range of activities in the British Embassy in St Luke. I will talk to Deputy Commissioner Sir Adrian Fitz-Hugh at Scotland Yard, who we met over our recent art investigations – he will know about Customs and so on himself, or put us onto someone who does. I don't think we should approach Sharpe directly, given that we are trying to keep Janice safe."

Melpomene asked Jimmy what the extra information was that he had mentioned before.

"Ah, yes. As you know, I'm a great believer in the value of surveillance in certain situations, so I arranged for the embassy and houses in Yeominster Square to be watched – not 24 hours a day, but at frequent intervals during daylight hours. One of my blokes, pretending to be a commercial traveller, took a furnished room in a block of apartments almost opposite the main embassy building, with a powerful pair of German binoculars and one of those miniature Leica cameras. And other members of my team might have been observed from time to time playing with their dogs in the gardens in the centre of the square, and I even had Detective-Constable Valerie Morton, outfitted as a nursemaid, pushing a pram around the square – with a dressed-up doll in it, not a baby! And I took a leaf out of your book, Melpomene, and worked my way round all the houses in the square as an estate agent, asking if each house was available for rental. Of course I got a variety of reactions, including rude ones, but some patiently pointed out that these were diplomatic properties."

"And did they volunteer anything useful, Jimmy?" asked Melpomene, "or did they just clam up?"

"You might be surprised how informative a carefully buttered-up house-maid can be, especially when she is bored!" said Jimmy, "I got the full names of all of the people in the house sometimes, together with their functions, hobbies and tastes in music! For example, Brigadier Douglas was described as being in charge of all the guards at the embassy, and as a 'wonderful violinist', while his wife 'does nothing but read magazines in bed all day, ringing for tea every ten minutes and complaining that the room is too hot or too cold'! I made copious shorthand notes – I'll leave them for you. Can Winnie or Marjorie do Gregg as well as Pitman?" "No problem, Jimmy, Alex can transcribe Gregg – he was taught it at Law School! What about the other watchers – were they able to pick up much?"

"Once again, Melpomene, I've had their daily reports for the week collated and typed up – here is a copy for you to have and peruse. One item I'll bring to your attention, because I have a feeling it might be significant. One of the official embassy houses, occupied, as I found out, by the chief Chancery clerk – his rank, I'm told, is higher than his modest title might indicate – is opposite one of the gates to the gardens in the square. Regularly, at 11 am and 4 pm, a maid goes into the park and meets a young man, whom she greets affectionately. All right, you say, even maids can have a love life! But not every maid passes a thick buff envelope to her beau in the morning and receives a similar one in the afternoon! Before you ask me – yes, I did have him followed! After the morning meeting, he hastens to a coffee-shop in a street adjacent to the square, orders coffee and a pastry, sits at a quiet table, opens the envelope and goes through the contents, making pencil notes on the papers inside before replacing them. Then he addresses the envelope, takes a stamp from his wallet, and posts it in a pillar-box near by!"

"Tell me, Jimmy," asked Alex, who had been listening intently, "Have the police the powers to intercept mail and open it? Or even to get a look at such envelopes and read the address?"

"The short answer, Alex, is 'Yes' – but only under extreme circumstances and with a search warrant sworn out by a senior judge. Since this is venturing into the realm of diplomatic immunity, it would probably be impossible without Foreign Office approval. However if underhand methods were used …!"

Chapter 18

Melpomene and Alex thanked Jimmy warmly, Mel saying, "Now we have an abundance of leads – but this brings up the problem of choosing one to start with. Perhaps we ought to divide the tasks between us, Alex, what do you say? I'm inclined to telephone Walter and see if he can suggest who to start talking to about money transactions – presumably the Comptroller's office deals only with legitimate transfers, whereas anyone who is trying to do some dishonest business on the side would avoid processing their deals through official channels."

"Desmond McPhail would be a useful first contact," said Alex, "Walter has known him for years and trusts him, and Elizabeth O'Connor told me she often works with him. Maybe he has twigged that sometimes she makes a bit on the side. Why not try him, if Walter agrees?"

Jimmy excused himself at that point, saying that he felt he ought to show himself at the station from time to time, "Some of the uniform branch have the view that we members of CID are on long-term holidays, spending our time having beers with crims in low-class pubs – they have a point, of course, but we try not to reinforce this idea too much! Let me know how matters progress, and I'll keep you in the picture, too!"

Marjorie got Walter Huskisson on the telephone for Melpomene, who opened by thanking him for inviting them to the celebration. "Besides enjoying the meal and general chit-chat, we had lots of interesting conversations, Walter. By the way, I have been wondering about something – perhaps you wouldn't mind enlightening me. It seems that almost all of the embassy staff – the ones we met, anyway – are not citizens of St Luke, but British – is that an accurate assumption?"

"Certainly, Melpomene, in fact there are only five St Luke nationals at the embassy – the Ambassador, Chevalier Dominique de Chapelle and his wife Héloïse, the head of chancery, M Marcel Lavalier, the comptroller, Mr Cyril Sidmouth, and the chief of protocol, M Alain du Pont. Everyone else is locally employed, like me. The reason for this is simply the size of the nation – St Luke has a total population of less than two million, and, regrettably, a large proportion of those are uneducated or illiterate, meaning that the pool of suitable people for staffing overseas missions is rather small. St Luke maintains only three permanent Embassies – in London, Paris and Washington – and is represented in other countries by offices of varying degrees of importance, helped out by businessmen and others with special interests."

"So your old friend, Desmond McPhail, works under Mr Sidmouth – have I got it right?"

"That is correct, Mel, but Cyril Sidmouth, as it happens, has relatively modest accountancy qualifications – from a community college in Florida, USA, I believe – so he tends to rely heavily on Desmond, who is an honours graduate of the University of Edinburgh Business School and a Chartered Accountant."

Melpomene continued, "I was wondering whether to ask Mr McPhail if he could help me to track down whatever incident it was that prompted the accusations of illegal activities at the British Embassy in St Luke. Your colleague, Elizabeth O'Connor is behaving rather suspiciously, in my view – I'm convinced she lied about leaking that story to the Sunday newspaper – and she seemed to be on good terms with Desmond at the restaurant, even telling Alex that he had helped her with enquiries about financial matters from time to time and suggesting that Alex might approach him too!"

"Please go ahead, Melpomene," said Walter, "I am confident that you will behave with appropriate discretion! I've known Desmond for years, as I believe I've told you – he is an honest and above-board person! Is there anything else I can tell you for now?"

"Just one more thing, Walter. What happens to incoming mail – just Post Office deliveries, not diplomatic bag stuff – I assume some families get their mail delivered directly to their homes, while a lot intended for individuals and addressed to the embassy is handled by a mail room or some such. Is that right? Is it all opened and scrutinised, or what?"

"Quite right, Mel, this is how it works. If there is a letter addressed to W Huskisson, Esq., 12 Yeominster Square, it just gets put through our front door by the postman. If a letter is addressed to W Huskisson, Third Secretary (Commerce), Embassy of St Luke, Yeominster Square, it is delivered, usually with a bagful of other mail, directly to the embassy, where it is taken to our mail room and sorted. After a day or two, it eventually reaches me, opened and rubber-stamped "Mail Checked", so the mail officer obviously reads everything before passing it on. Some items get passed first to other officers, who initial them, occasionally adding notes, and send them on their way. Once in a while, I have been called by a senior officer and asked to explain something."

"Thanks very much, Walter, I can now speak to Desmond McPhail a little more confidently! I'll let you know if I come up with anything, of course."

Mel rang off and said to Alex, "Once you've had a chance to decipher Jimmy's notes. I'll see what they say about the McPhail household and then I can decide how to proceed. I shall probably be interviewing him at his home – it would cause too much comment if I went to the embassy, and I'm not even sure whether they let outsiders in, as a general rule. And although it is always pleasant to talk to someone in a café or pub, our present business needs a more secure situation. As I know from doing it myself, any one who can lip-read can pick up a lot from across a noisy room."

"It sounds as though you have your work planned out for a while, Mel," said Alex, "Meanwhile I shall be pursuing a different line. I shall approach Deputy Commissioner Fitz-Hugh at Scotland Yard – he covers much the same territory as Jens-Olle Pedersen and Hugo Palance and while we were concentrating on art-related matters with them before, we know that they don't limit themselves to that alone, but have general interests in illicit traffic of all kinds, such as gun smuggling and rum-running."

Mel reminded him, "And since we have just found that St Luke maintains an embassy in Paris, we ought to get in touch with Commissaire Principal Palance as well – I'm sure the Sûreté has a hand in investigating diplomatic business of an illicit nature. Knowing Hugo, he will be keen to enliven his day-to-day work!"

"Right, my darling, I will proceed on those lines. Are there any more people we are supposed to be ringing? Perhaps we should ask one of you, Marjorie or Winnie, to set up a proper engagement diary, including telephone enquiries. We are gradually becoming more organised here at Crabbe and Crabbe, are we not? Almost like a well-conducted business!"

Chapter 19

Melpomene announced that it felt like lunchtime, to which Alex replied, "It always feels like lunchtime for you, Mel! But let's go to Guiseppe's and see what he has on his lunch menu today."

Mel grabbed the notes that Jimmy had brought, and once they were seated in the trattoria awaiting Alex' order of *polpi alla griglia* and Mel's choice of *gnocchi alla gorgonzola*, she leafed through the pages until she found one headed "No. 18 – McPhail", which listed Desmond McPhail, his wife Morag and their daughter Phillipa, aged 3. Their staff seemed modest, consisting of a cook-housekeeper, a housemaid and a nanny. Jimmy had commented that the maid who answered the door to him had been polite but dismissive, saying that the house belonged to the embassy and was unavailable, but volunteering that 'the madam' had been complaining that they would soon need somewhere larger – "I think she might be in the family way again, but nobody is supposed to know!"

Jimmy had kept in character, telling the girl that she should contact him at Staples and Staples estate agents in Kensington High Street if she thought that the McPhails were about to start looking for places seriously. He had then apologized for not having a card to leave her, as he had run out.

Mel made a mental note to steer clear of these topics unless Desmond raised them himself, but that it was useful information nevertheless.

Back in the office after lunch, Mel telephoned the embassy and asked to speak to Mr McPhail. She was put through without being asked to identify herself, which struck her as slightly surprising, and was soon talking to a woman who announced, "Comptroller's Office, Beryl Harrison here." Once again, Mel was not asked who she was, but was soon talking to Desmond McPhail, saying, "I don't know whether you will remember me from the Huskissons' celebration last Saturday, Mr McPhail – my name is Melpomene Crabbe – we only spoke briefly – I was the not very tall blonde person in dark green velvet."

"Oh, yes, I remember you, Mrs Crabbe – I recall that later you were having a long serious discussion with Cedric Douglas – he seems to develop an immediate fascination with any attractive girl that he encounters at a gathering."

"Thank you, kind sir, she said!" replied Mel, "The reason I'm telephoning is to see whether you could spare me some time one evening, preferably at your house, so I can ask you a few questions about embassy procedures in general and about some specific topics dealing with a matter that Walter Huskisson has asked us to look into. I am one half of the firm of Crabbe and Crabbe, Private Investigators, and my husband Alex is the other. Perhaps you recall him too – he is tall, dark and handsome – and I'm not the only one of that opinion!"

"It will be my pleasure!" said McPhail, "Would this evening be too soon – shall we say 7.30? I say that because my wife and I have semi-official engagements for tomorrow and the day after. We tend to dine rather early most days, so we can enjoy the company at table of our little girl, who is becoming more and more civilized with every passing week – she stopped throwing food at us some months ago!"

"I look forward to meeting you all this evening!" said Mel, and she rang off, saying to Alex, "Desmond McPhail sounds quite like a human being! Have you had any luck contacting Deputy Commissioner Fitz-Hugh?"

"His assistant said he would ring back – he's in a meeting now. So I just told him who I was and said that my query was possibly to do with illicit international transfers of money or goods but that I would appreciate the chance to meet with the Deputy Commissioner and discuss it properly. We shall see! Perhaps in the meantime I should try Hugo Palance. Marjorie – can you see if you can get him for me, please?"

Marjorie spoke to the operator, and then said that there would be about ten minutes to wait for a cross-channel line.

Melpomene decided that before going out she would drive back to the flat and grab a quick snack, saying, "I'm glad we had a substantial luncheon! I shall be going to the McPhails after their dinner-time so I might feel a bit peckish by the time I'm finished there! Do you want to come with me in the car, Alex, or will you go by the underground?"

"Don't worry, Mel, I don't know how long I will be tied up on various telephone calls now. See you tonight! By the way, since you will be on your own in a secluded neighbourhood, you should take your little Beretta with you – loaded and cocked, with the safety on, as Jimmy always advises!"

Melpomene was ringing the bell at Number 18, Yeominster Square at precisely 7.30. She was welcomed in by a maid, and taken to a sitting-room, to find Desmond and Morag, his wife, playing with their little daughter, who was already in her night clothes. Phillipa kissed her mummy and daddy and came to Melpomene for a hug and a kiss too, before her nanny came to put her to bed.

"You've seen us both at the restaurant, Melpomene – may I call you that?" said Desmond, "But we didn't have a chance for a chat then. Because you've come here on business tonight, however, we'd better get straight down to brass tacks. Morag, my love, perhaps you can join us later and we can have a cup of chocolate or something."

Morag took her leave, shaking hands, and Mel and Desmond settled down on comfortable chairs, Mel explaining that she had a somewhat hypothetical question for him to start with. "Suppose I were an officer in this embassy who wanted to send something not quite legal – for example, some drugs or a firearm – to an acquaintance in another embassy overseas, under cover of a diplomatic bag. Could I manage this? And if so, how would I go about it? And who else would need to be involved?"

"Well, Mel, it would first depend on your status here. We have privileges depending on our rank and position. The Ambassador, the chief of protocol and the comptroller need nobody's approval to, for instance, initiate a diplomatic bag with undisclosed contents, whereas others are limited to sums of money for specified purposes and documents clearly related to their function, approved by their chief – in my case, the comptroller."

Mel persisted, "So, Desmond, are the contents examined thoroughly before the bag is sealed?"

Desmond grinned, "They are *supposed* to be, of course, but it doesn't always happen according to the book. The sealing is done by a designated clerk, who has charge of the lead seals we use, and of the sealing pliers, but often he has several bags in front of him, and it would be possible – *and is* possible – to slip an extra item or two into one of them while he is not paying attention! I must admit – and this is highly confidential, of course – that I have even done this myself in order to send friends little gifts for birthdays and so on!"

Chapter 20

"I understand, Desmond – even Homer nods!" said Melpomene. "Now, a further question. All of you at the embassy are in one or more sets of relationships that depend, amongst other matters, on function, personality and history, as my study of social anthropology tells me! And these are often accompanied by expectations and even obligations."

"I think I follow you," said Desmond, "I would do something for a friend that I wouldn't for someone else, and I would 'play it by the book' for someone I don't get on with. Is that the sort of thing you mean?"

"You've got it, Desmond! And now I am going to get down to cases. I will not be violating any confidences if I tell you that Walter Huskisson has become concerned about certain folk in the embassy who have apparently been spending more than they earn – or at least have been behaving more extravagantly than one might expect. His concern has reached a level which has induced him to go to the police, who in turn have called upon our detective agency. Maybe you have picked this up already, yourself. So, let us be blunt – are you aware of any of your colleagues who have been 'working the system' as it were?"

"Like Walter, I have had suspicions, Melpomene, but as for evidence that would stand up in court, that is a different thing. However, I did have a very interesting experience about six months ago, concerning our press attaché. I believe your husband had a conversation with her last Saturday evening when the so-called 'leak' to that Sunday rag was mentioned. I can provide some elucidation here, but what it reveals is not improper dealings within the embassy, or between this embassy and others, but a plain case of fraudulent conduct, or, if you like, of selling false information. Elizabeth O'Connor, I believe is being paid large sums by the Trumpet – and other unprincipled newspapers – to construct plausible stories out of gossip and hearsay. What happened was this – one of the long-term officers in our division resigned to move into his family brokerage firm, merely looking for a change in occupation. Within a week, his photograph appeared in two of the popular papers, along with a news item implying that he had been dismissed for embezzlement. You can imagine how this might have affected his new career!"

"Didn't he take any action against the papers?" asked Melpomene.

"He came and saw me, as an old colleague, and I advised him to seek legal advice before he did anything. The upshot was that he was advised that the articles were worded so obscurely that an action would be unlikely to succeed, besides which the newspapers have access to huge funds and would engage top barristers, so he shrugged and simply waited for it all to blow over. His new colleagues were mostly family, so they had full confidence in him."

"And you think this was Elizabeth O'Connor's doing?"

"I'm sure of it! In order to spice up the articles, the name of the account from which he was alleged to have been siphoning funds was given – but this was a fictitious account with a name I had made up myself as an example for Elizabeth when she was asking me how the system here at the embassy worked!"

"Are you going to take this higher, Desmond?"

"Yes, Melpomene, I certainly intend to, but as an accountant I feel the need to be meticulous in presenting my evidence to the comptroller and the chief of protocol, both of whom should know of my suspicions. I have started to compile a dossier about O'Connor and also about Douglas, the military attaché, who I have not mentioned so far, but who I feel has been perpetrating dishonest activity at a far more serious level. If you'll forgive me, Melpomene, I won't go into that with you now, but I promise to be much more forthcoming when I am more certain of my facts. Suffice to say that I believe Cedric Douglas is guilty, not only of breaches of diplomatic protocol, but of criminal activity of the most grave kind!"

"I must thank you, Desmond, most sincerely for what you have given me so far!" said Melpomene, grasping his hand.

"My pleasure, Mel, and I feel some relief in being able to share these facts with someone who will use them properly! Now, let us have some refreshments and some pleasant chatter with Morag! I will go and fetch her."

Morag McPhail turned out to be someone who Melpomene would like to have as a permanent friend, being interested in many of the same topics as she – tennis, the movies, cryptic crosswords and even sports cars!

Mel took this as an opportunity to brag about her new Riley and to reminisce about her dear departed Alvis, while Morag was saying that she had been trying to get Desmond to replace their rather staid Wolseley by something along the lines of an MG, a Lancia or even an Alfa Romeo – at which Melpomene's eyes shone – and soon the two were engaged in a technical discussion.

"Have you come across the pre-selector gearbox?" asked Mel, "Our new Riley has one, and I'm getting quite keen on it, although it took a bit of getting used to if you are an experienced driver with the crash box. When I forget, I find myself using the left pedal like a clutch, while it really just engages whatever gear you selected last. Maybe I'll give you a demonstration some day – but not tonight, it's getting a bit late!"

Such pleasant conversation continued until Mel, noticing the time, got up and made her farewells.

"Can I walk you to your car, Mel?" asked Desmond, to which she replied, "No need, Desmond, thanks very much, it's parked right by your front gate!"

A few minutes later she was to regret this decision!

She walked to the driver's side and took her seat, tucking her handbag by her side. She started up and drove around the square toward one of the two roads that gave onto the main street that would take her home, but while she was still in the square, she felt something cold pressing into the back of her neck, and a gruff voice said from the back seat, "Just keep on driving, darling, and make no sudden movements! I'll tell you where to go! Just drive slow, like you are now, I'll tell you what turns to take in plenty of time!"

She was directed to take the main road, and when they reached it, to go in the opposite direction she needed to take to get home. She recovered her voice, intentionally making herself sound scared stiff, although her mind was really working overtime, while saying, "Where are you taking me, I don't like this at all!"

"Just shut up and do what I say!" said the man, still pressing the pistol or whatever it was against her neck.

Chapter 21

Soon they were in an area that Melpomene didn't recognize at all, though she guessed they were travelling north. Her new acquaintance was holding onto the back of the passenger's seat, craning forward, trying to look for landmarks, and muttering under his breath the names of the streets as he saw the signs. As she drove, Mel felt in her handbag for her Beretta, slipped off the safety and wedged it on the seat under her thigh. They passed a corner where people were streaming out of a pub, and she got a glimpse of the sign, "The Builders Arms", which she thought she would try to remember. Then her companion growled, "Turn left just past that Police Box."

She found they were now in a gloomy laneway, behind a row of houses or shops. There were dustbins lined up along the back wall. The man said, "Take it steady, I'm going to come over and join you!" and started to climb over onto the passenger's seat. Mel quietly selected reverse gear, and saw that the man, who was wearing a long raincoat, was having to use both hands, even the one with the pistol, to steady himself. As he was half way over, she stamped down hard with both feet on the gear change and brake pedals, bringing the car to a shuddering stop in a squeal of tyres.

He pitched forward in a heap, with his head and shoulders nearly on the floor in front of the seat and Mel saw that he had lost his grip on his gun, which had fallen to the floor. As he reached for it, Melpomene grasped her Beretta and shot him through the back of his outstretched hand, saying "Try that again and I'll drop you!"

The man shrieked in pain and tried to staunch the profuse bleeding with his other hand. He had given up any thoughts of using the gun, but huddled on the seat, moaning and rocking, while he wrapped his injured hand with his white silk scarf. Melpomene was taking no chances, so she hooked his pistol along the floor with her foot, grabbed it and stowed it in her coat pocket, noting with approval that it was a Luger, like the one that Alex had!

The man had stopped moaning now, so, still aiming the gun at him, Mel reached over with her left hand and raised his eyelid.

There was no response, so she thought, "Either I've killed him or he's passed out! In any case, I need help."

She started the engine, which had stalled during the crash stop, selected first gear and turned around in the lane, proud of the neatness of her three-point turn. She drove slowly to the beginning of the lane, keeping an eye on the man who was still not moving, though she could see, thankfully, that he was breathing, however shallowly.

It was only a few steps to the police phone box and Mel went up and opened the little door to the telephone compartment, lifted the earpiece off the hook and waited for a response. A male voice answered, "Metropolitan Police here, which service do you require?"

Mel said, "An ambulance, first of all, and then the police, I have an injured criminal here. I am at your box on the corner of Leslie Street and Wilkes Lane, the man is passed out in a Riley car parked nearby. I will go back to the car and keep an eye on him in case he regains consciousness – he threatened me with a pistol earlier."

"Thank you Madam," replied the operator, in an impressively calm voice, "who am I speaking to?"

"My name is Melpomene Crabbe, I will give you my full details when this is all taken care of."

"No need, Mrs Crabbe – your name is known throughout the Force!" said the operator, chuckling – I am Sergeant Cliffe – give my regards to Inspector Manley when you see him next!"

She heard the bell of an approaching ambulance almost as soon as she got back to the Riley. The occupant was still not moving, but she kept the Beretta ready. When the ambulance men arrived, they had to open the door carefully, supporting the man, otherwise he would have fallen onto the ground. They lifted him onto a stretcher and took him to the ambulance, one of them saying to Melpomene, "We are taking him to Emergency at Finchley Hospital, he looks as if he'll need a transfusion pretty soon if we are to save him! You can follow us if you like. Is he a relative, Madam?"

Just then, a policeman arrived on his bicycle, and when the situation had been explained to him, said, "I'll ride with this lady and direct her to the hospital, so off you go. Let me chain my bike to this lamp-post first, Madam. If I get it pinched I shall have to make out endless reports!"

Mel said, "You had better travel in the back seat, unless you want to spoil your uniform with a lot of blood! Looks as though I shall need new floor mats at the least! I'll tell you what happened as we go, if you want to write it down in your book!"

At the hospital, the unconscious man was taken to a treatment room while a clerk started to take down the particulars. The policeman, PC Savage, had been through the criminal's pockets and proceed to go through his wallet and an opened envelope from the same pocket.

"According to his driving licence, his name is Tony Pinson, but we will take this with a grain of salt – I've not met a villain yet who went by his real name. A couple of quid and a book of stamps are the only other things here. Once he's been printed we'll know a lot more, of course – I'd bet you anything you like he's a habitual offender. Let's see what this letter is."

PC Savage read through the letter, and then shook his head and passed it to Melpomene, "See if you can make anything of this, Madam, it doesn't mean much to me!"

Mel sat down heavily on one of the chairs in front of the hospital counter, and the attendant said, to an assistant, "Get this lady a cup of strong sweet tea quickly – she looks as though she's having a reaction to all the excitement!"

Indeed, Mel was feeling somewhat faint, but the tea and a Nice biscuit soon made her feel a bit better, and she started to peruse the letter.

The attendant then said, "Is there anyone we should telephone, Madam? I don't think you should be driving yet."

Melpomene said, "Oh yes, of course – I'd better let my husband know about all this – he'll be worried about me – what time is it? I should have been home a couple of hours ago!"

Alex did sound rather anxious on the telephone, and Mel explained that there had been some excitement, but that she was all right, if a trifle woozy. He asked exactly where she was and said he would take a taxi and be with her as soon as possible.

"I'll tell you the rest as soon as I see you!" she said, "Don't rush!"

Chapter 22

Half an hour later, still waiting for Alex to arrive, Melpomene had tried to read the letter, which was, as PC Savage had said, not easy to understand. She worked out that it was using a lot of private references – not exactly code, but words that wouldn't mean a lot to anyone not in the know. It seemed to be instructions, and Mel assumed it to be the orders given to her assailant by a superior. Using techniques not unlike those she had found useful when doing crosswords, she started to write out a few phrases.

She murmured them aloud, at first just for her own benefit, but found that the PC was eagerly listening, wanting to understand too, so she started addressing him.

"It says 'the notorious lady', which I can only assume must refer to me, however inappropriate it may sound. And later on, there is the phrase 'you may need help from cleaning services' – maybe these are members of the gang who deal with difficult cases, I don't know! But when it gets to 'cabinet maker' and 'whistler' I'm baffled!"

PC Savage spoke up, "I've known crims who were identified by their original trades, like 'cobbler' and 'grocer' – perhaps these are similar. Unfortunately this doesn't help us, as outsiders!"

"The other bit that confuses me," Mel continued, "is where it says 'after the event, disregard reactions, simply go back' – what can that imply? Does he mean 'after you've killed her' – or 'if she escapes' – there's no way of knowing! And it is addressed to 'B' and the signature is 'Grannie' or 'Graham' – the writing is terrible! Very puzzling! Maybe Alex will have some ideas – he should be here by now, surely?"

As if in answer, Alex appeared at the door, said, "Impossible to get a taxi at this time of night! Are you all right, my dear?" and gave her a hug.

Just then, a doctor came from the inner rooms, saying, "One more saved! It took at least two pints of blood and some chest massage to bring him round, and he's still not fully conscious, but he'll live! Are you the relatives? He seems to have taken a bullet to the hand – I've saved it for the police. It had broken two bones in the back of his hand and severed a large blood-vessel, hence the profuse bleeding! Would somebody like to tell me what this is all about?"

Melpomene said, "I'll tell you all, to save time, but it's a bit public here, isn't it? Is there somewhere nearby we can sit?"

The doctor introduced himself as Gordon Salmon, and led them to a treatment room. He perched on the edge of the bed there and PC Savage, Alex and Melpomene took the three chairs.

Mel started by introducing herself and Alex – Doctor Salmon was obviously intrigued to be dealing with detectives, while the policemen nodded knowingly – he had apparently heard of them, like the telephone operator earlier.

She then proceeded to relate the whole sequence of events, from leaving the house – she did not say whose house it was, nor why she had been there – until arriving at the hospital just after the injured man. PC Savage was scribbling everything down in his notebook, occasionally asking for clarification.

"You must be a crack shot!" he said admiringly when Mel told of shooting the man. "Not really!" she said, "there was only a few inches between my gun and the man's hand when I fired! But, come to think of it, I'm not bad anyway – on the indoor practice range at Mile End Road police station, I can shoot a magazine-full and make a group no bigger than three inches or so across!"

Doctor Salmon interjected, "That's as maybe, the fact remains that you got him exactly where it would put him out of action fastest – I've known patients to walk into my surgery with a broken arm thinking they just had a bruise! – but it was as much the pain as well as the loss of blood that knocked this man out. By the way, officer, I called the local police station and they have sent someone to sit with him in a locked ward until he's recovered enough to be charged and put away. In this part of town, it's not all that unusual for us to be treating criminals. I had a couple in last week who'd cut each other up with kitchen knives in a local café kitchen! Mostly superficial cuts but they still needed lots of stitches!"

Alex noticed that Mel was starting to nod off, so he said briskly, "Come along, Madam, we'd better get you home." He thanked the doctor for his time, and said that no doubt the local police would want to talk more to Melpomene about the whole incident soon.

He took Mel by the arm and led her back to the Riley. He was just about to help her into the passenger's seat when she roused herself and said, "Back seat, please, my love, there's gore all over the front one!"

Back at the flat, he helped her to her bath, made her a cup of chocolate and saw she was comfortable in bed. Within two minutes she was fast asleep.

First thing next morning, Melpomene, fresh as ever, telephoned Jimmy Manley and related the tale once again, finally saying, "You should ring the emergency department at Finchley hospital. And they will tell you whether the man has been taken into custody and where. If PC Savage was right, he is a habitual offender, so his prints should be on file and we shall find out a lot more about him. I've been puzzling over this letter, Jimmy, I'll read it out to you and you can see whether you can make any more sense out of it than I can. Here goes, it's addressed just to 'B', no 'Dear' or anything, and it goes on, *'Wait outside No. 18 and do nothing till she's in the car and driving away. Her car is a Riley tourer, so if the doors are locked you'll be able to get in by slitting the hood. Hide in the back seat and wait for her. Whistler will tip you the wink when she comes out. You'll recognize the notorious lady by her blonde curls, anyway. You know where to bring her – take no chances, keep your gun on her, she's a tricky one. When you get to the shed, you may need help from cleaning services. Cabinet maker will be there, too, but don't take your eye off her for a second. After the event, disregard reactions, simply go back. Grannie.'* (that could be 'Graham'), I can't tell which. Mean anything to you, Jimmy?"

"Not a great deal, Melpomene!" replied Jimmy, "I don't recognize any of the names – they don't seem to be the monickers of any crims I've come across, anyway. I'll call Finchley hospital – but most likely they took him to Finchley North nick – might try telephoning there first, to save a bit of time. I'll get back to you as soon as I get something on your Mr Pinson, or whatever his real name is."

When Jimmy had rung off, Alex had an idea, "I've been wondering how these bad persons found out about your movements. I think I might ring Walter at home – it's probably early enough to catch him – and ask him what he knows about the woman who runs the switch at the embassy. As far as I can work out, she would be the only one who knew you had telephoned Walter yesterday, apart from Morag, of course."

Chapter 23

Walter Huskisson had not yet left for work when Alex telephoned and was quite happy to talk. Alex told him that Melpomene's meeting with Desmond McPhail had been satisfactory up to a point, prompting Walter to ask what he meant. "She got some useful information about the ways that diplomatic bags are managed, which will be useful background for future enquiries, and Desmond was very forthcoming about his suspicions – and actual information – about Elizabeth O'Connor and her shifty dealings with the press. We shall talk to Desmond some more – he is going to be a valuable resource inside the embassy. Mel left in quite a satisfied mood – but this was very soon upset!"

"Why, what happened?" asked Walter.

"She got into her car all right, and was just starting when a man hidden in the back seat put a pistol to her neck and forced her to drive off! This, as it turned out, was not just an attempt at robbery – we found out later he was working to orders and intended to deliver Mel to some sort of gang hide-out. But, my dear Melpomene is made of sterner stuff and was not prepared to be pushed about like that! To cut a long story short, she shot him in the hand and he finished up in an unconscious state and on his way to hospital by ambulance!"

"Amazing! So who was this man and who was he working for – do you know yet?"

"Not yet, but he was patched up at the hospital and is now in custody. The police think that he is a habitual criminal, so once he's been finger-printed they will be able to find out much more from Criminal Records. We haven't heard yet. But Walter, aside from letting you know all this, I telephoned for a particular purpose. It seems clear that Melpomene was expected by these crooks to be at Desmond's house – and this information could only have come from the embassy! My suspicions are firstly of the woman who operates the telephone switchboard – I don't know her name but she would be in a position to listen in on Mel's conversation with Desmond – and secondly, I have just realized, there is someone called Beryl Harrison, who seems to be a secretary in the Comptroller's department, who Mel spoke to as well. I can't think of any other possible people who could have leaked the information, can you? What do you think of these ideas? What do you know about these two women?"

"The daytime switch operator's name is Phyllis – I don't know her surname, but it would be easy to find – but I really know nothing about her – she is just one of those disembodied voices who are accepted as part of the equipment, I'm afraid. There is a man who works the switchboard at night, from 8pm to 8am, and I know nothing about him either, not even his name – not that this is at all relevant, I suppose. I have met Miss Harrison on one or two semi-social occasions, and I sometimes have dealings with her on matters of business, but you should ask Desmond, he works much more closely with her, of course, being in the same division. Perhaps you should see him at home to avoid eaves-dropping, just as you have telephoned here to speak to me now."

"You are right, Walter – I'm beginning to think that your embassy is dangerous territory!"

"I really feel quite guilty that I have drawn you into all this, Alex, especially in exposing Melpomene to what must have been real danger! I never thought it would lead to this when I first went to the police! I should quite understand it if you wish to withdraw from the case!"

"Just try to stop me and Melpomene now that we've got the bit between our teeth, Walter! This is bread-and-butter for Crabbe and Crabbe! I had better let you get to work – I'll certainly be talking to you again. Give my regards to Marie-Colette!"

Melpomene had been listening to all this, and said, "As soon as we get to the office, we should see if Deputy Commissioner Fitz-Hugh is available now – I take it that he didn't return your call yesterday?"

"Not really, Mel – his secretary apologized for him and said that he had been called away, but would be in tomorrow – that's today now, of course. I'll try him as soon as we get there."

At the office, Winnie told them that they had received several calls already, including one from Jimmy Manley, saying that he had tried them at home first but was told by Caroline that they were on their way to the office. He had heard from Criminal Records and thought that Alex and Mel might be interested in what they had found out about the so-called Tony Pinson. So

Mel said she would call him back while Alex was telephoning Fitz-Hugh.

Jimmy said he was quite pleased with what he had ben told about 'Tony Pinson', "His real name is Reg Withers and he has a record going back to when he was twelve! His first few exploits then were shop-lifting – cigarettes and chocolates and such – but after a year in Borstal he came out with bigger ideas. He was locked up at age eighteen for burglary and GBH – grievous bodily harm – when he was disturbed by a woman as he was going through the drawers in her bedroom and bashed her with a candlestick. He got five years for that but was paroled after three for 'exemplary behaviour'. And so on and so on – since then he has spent more time locked up than out on the streets. He last came out from Pentonville in February last year and this is the first we've seen of him since then. We haven't been able to interview him yet, until the medicos give us the all clear, but I bet he's been working for the heavy mob – stand-over men I would think – we shall find out eventually."

Melpomene said, "So, according to that letter we found, it looks as though he was hired for my job – possibly through a gang, which I suppose is equivalent to an agency in our world! It would be good to find out just who – there are apparently members called Grannie – or Graham – Cabinet Maker and Whistler! And a department called 'Cleaning Services' – quite an organisation altogether, and it may be more extensive than that! But the most interesting person we need to find out about would be the client – assuming that this gang was engaged by someone or other to do something or other to me!"

Jimmy assured her that they would do their best to find all this out, "You've probably put the frights into him – all I'll have to do is threaten to hand him over to you and he'll squeal all right!"

When Melpomene hung up from Jimmy, Alex had also finished his call to the Deputy Commissioner.

"He would like us to go and meet with him at Scotland Yard later today, Mel. When I mentioned that we were dealing with diplomats he asked me several questions in quick succession. I wonder whether we shall find that we each have some of the same people in our sights. I didn't say anything to Fitz-Hugh, but I'm feeling more and more suspicious of Brigadier Cedric Douglas, our military attaché!"

Chapter 24

After lunch, Melpomene and Alex drove to Scotland Yard, telling the policeman on the gate that they had an appointment with Deputy Commissioner Fitz-Hugh. He was suitably impressed and showed them where to park, saying, "His office is on the ground floor, anyone will show you where. You can go in through that door and turn right."

Once inside they asked again and were shown to an unmarked door, which opened onto a reception area where a young woman in civilian clothes was sitting at a desk typing. As they entered, she stood up and said, "Mr and Mrs Crabbe? The Deputy Commissioner is expecting you," and opened a door to an inner office.

He got up from his desk and came to shake hands, saying, "Last time we met, we were concerned with those art gangs that you so comprehensively dealt with! By the way, I still owe you a celebratory dinner over that affair! I gather that this time we have progressed in the world and are moving in diplomatic circles! Come and sit down and tell me all about it, please. Would you like a tea or coffee?"

"Well," started Alex, "I hinted that this was all about possible illicit transfer of money or goods – possibly by way of diplomatic pouches. We have only suspicions to work on so far, but we strongly believe that a person or persons at the St Luke embassy are involved. Detective-Inspector Jimmy Manley at Mile End Road was called in by someone at the embassy in the first instance, and Jimmy thought that it was right up Crabbe and Crabbe's street."

"He was probably right!" said Fitz-Hugh, "I have great respect for that young man's judgment – he will go far in the force, I'm sure! Carry on, please."

Melpomene and Alex took turns in relating the whole story, starting with Phoebe's initial concerns about Janice and finishing with the attempted abduction. Fitz-Hugh listened intently, making notes on a pad from time to time. After a while, a woman in a white overall brought in a tray with tea-things and biscuits, and they all paused to sip and nibble. Then the Deputy Commissioner made some comments.

"First of all," he said, "I can quite believe your friend Huskisson's anecdotes about funny business with money from unknown sources. If there is a sizeable organization anywhere which is completely free of fiddles, I have yet to meet it. Embassies are no exception, and they offer better opportunities than most for illicit dealing, because of this almost religious attitude towards diplomatic privilege that surrounds them! At the trivial end of the scale, you might be surprised how often cars with 'CD' plates are seen illegally parked outside dubious night-clubs and worse!"

He took a sip of tea and continued, "As for these unusual displays of unwarranted wealth that your friend observed, my guess is that they stem from payments for services rendered. As you know, this special section of the Yard that I try to run is concerned with illicit international trade, and this includes smuggling and evasion of duty, the bribery of customs agents and port security officials, and even old-fashioned smuggling by small boats beaching on our shores on moonless nights. The illegitimate use of diplomatic bags is part of this whole grimy picture – but it relies on embassy staff who are prepared to ignore regulations for a price!"

Melpomene asked, "Have you got any suggestions about ways of testing our suspicions, Adrian – if I may call you by your first name – maybe we could set up a trap for Cedric Douglas to see whether we were right about him, what do you think?"

Fitz-Hugh frowned at this, but more in concentration than disapproval, Mel thought. After a while he said, slowly, "Even we police are unable to interfere with diplomatic bags sent in the mail, so I think we must rule out any attempt at checking them during transit. This means, clearly, that any checks have to be done before an item is dispatched, or after it has been received. I think you said, Melpomene, that your friend Desmond McPhail told you that there is a clerk at the embassy who is designated to attend to addressing and sealing diplomatic bags – do I recall that correctly?"

"That's right – Desmond actually admitted to slipping small items into bags while the clerk was not watching!"

"Good!" said Fitz-Hugh, "So we have McPhail and Huskisson inside the embassy who can discreetly keep an eye on things – of course, there is no chance that either of you will be let inside! But I'll tell you my gravest concern at the moment, which you may well have thought of, too – Inspector Manley as well. All that the 'gang' – we'll call them that for the want of a better description – knows at the moment is that friend Withers has disappeared and that Melpomene's abduction has failed. Sooner or later, one way or another, they will find out more. The 'client' – the person who recruited them for the job – is in a similar position. Once he or she finds out what happened, Melpomene will be in real danger! We should take serious steps before it is too late!"

Melpomene was alarmed, but not because of this danger – as she said, "I hope this does not mean that I'm to be banished to a convent and told not to stir until the coast is clear! However, I'm quite prepared to go into disguise and adopt a new identity – I've done it before and it worked for a while! And they seem to know all about our car, once again – I would be very peeved if they set fire to this one, as they did to our poor Alvis!"

Alex had been making notes while the others were talking and announced, "So it seems to me there are a number of tasks confronting us. Perhaps it would be a good idea to decide which of them is urgent and which can be put off for a while, as well as who should take responsibility for each of them. Here is my first attempt at a list. First, we need to interrogate Reg Withers as soon as he is *compos mentis*, to find out what we can about the gang – of course he may not know much, he is probably just a bit player. I'm sure that Jimmy Manley and his boys are the best suited to this. In a way, it's a shame that Mel never got taken as far as their 'shed' – this might have provided us with some useful evidence – but on the other hand she certainly did the right thing!"

"Thank you Alex, I'm glad you approve!" said Melpomene, but it could be seen that she hadn't taken offence.

Alex returned to his notes "The 'client' is the next major target. My fancy for this role is Cedric Douglas, as you can imagine. But he is a very fly character and to rise to the rank of Brigadier indicates he is not short of an organizational brain-cell or two. And anyone who works as a Military Attaché must be of dubious and devious character, in my view!"

Mel added, "But don't forget that Janice's father is one, too!"

"Yes – he's another bird to watch closely! For your information, Adrian, he is in the British Embassy in St Luke, and was the target of Elizabeth O'Connor's snide piece in The Trumpet!"

Chapter 25

Deputy Commissioner Adrian Fitz-Hugh continued "Have you any concrete evidence that brings you to conclude that Douglas is suspect, or are you just letting your personal feelings take over? From what you have told me, he does sound like the sort of person who is capable of engaging underworld figures to do his bidding, but I'm afraid that, as a policeman, I need a great deal more than that before I can take action! Maybe your friends Walter Huskisson and Desmond McPhail could keep a watch on him to see whether they can come up with any facts! But until we do pin him down – or whoever else it was who engaged Reg Withers or his controllers – we have to make sure that Melpomene is kept safe – you won't always be in a position to shoot someone, Mel, however alert you keep yourself!"

"So will it really come down to hiding myself away?" said Mel, looking downcast, "I think I would find that very hard to take! What about my idea of disguising myself and adopting an alias? Couldn't this be done?"

"In a way, Mel," said Fitz-Hugh, "have you ever heard of a witness protection programme? Some countries, particularly the United States, have well-established Federal procedures to counter intimidation of witnesses by organized crime, but in Britain this is left to local police forces. I'll talk to Jimmy Manley, and see whether he and his local station can come up with a suitable scheme – or I could even persuade my senior colleagues at Scotland Yard to do something similar. Leave it with me, Melpomene, and in the meantime don't go anywhere without Alex or some other burly person – and both of you should carry your pistols at all times! By the way, before it slips my mind, you mentioned someone in the British Embassy in St Luke, did you say he was the father of a young friend?"

"That's right, Adrian," said Mel, " He is Colonel Lionel Sharpe. Incidentally, his daughter Janice tells us that he is intending to ask for a transfer out of St Luke, with the pretext that he is concerned about his wife's health, which doesn't appear to be the case, since Janice has been assured by her mother that she is in good health!"

"This is all very interesting, Mel and Alex, since I have been tipped the wink about this man by an old acquaintance of mine at the Foreign Office! Let me ring for more tea, this is going to be quite a story!"

The woman in the overall responded quite quickly to the bell, and said, "Do you just want tea, Commissioner, or shall I bring sandwiches and such? Your guests may be getting peckish by now!"

Mel laughed, saying, "What a good idea!" so Adrian said "Thanks, Mrs Polson, that would be very nice!"

"Now I'll relate my history to you two!" he went on, "I came into the Met via what they call the graduate entry route. Instead of working my way up gradually, from being a humble copper on the beat, I went to Police College as a probationary Inspector, straight out of Oxford, where I had read PPE – that's Philosophy, Politics and Economics, which is a very popular choice for those destined for the public service. And at Oxford, I met Howard Anderson, who finished up in the Foreign Office, and we have kept in touch ever since. And it was at his initiative that he let me know about Lionel Sharpe. Please help yourselves to sandwiches – it looks as though there is a choice between cucumber, bloater paste and curried egg!"

"So, Adrian, what is the official lowdown on Colonel Sharpe?" asked Mel.

"Well, his misconduct seems to lie somewhere in between, on the one hand, the story that made the Sunday press, that he is involved in massive illegal currency transfers to the Bahamas and, on the other, fairly petty use of diplomatic bags for private purposes, such as having small items of jewellery bought by contacts in London as presents for Sharpe's lady friends in St Luke – of which, Howard Anderson tells me, he is not lacking! If the second of these is the case, it is still sufficient ground for dismissal, although, apparently, misdemeanours at that level are usually hushed up. Hence the story about his wife's ill-health, which might finish up as the public explanation. I will follow this up with Howard and let you know anything of importance that comes up."

"Thank you very much for all this, Adrian," said Alex, "what we must do now is first ensure Mel's safety, and second talk to Walter Huskisson and Desmond McPhail about what lines of enquiry they might follow. By the way, we have already resolved to avoid the Embassy telephones, as we have misgivings about their security – we shall do all our conversing to their home numbers. I have just remembered one more thing – sorry to rabbit on, Adrian!"

"Not to worry, Alex, carry on, please."

Alex did so, "Jimmy Manley observed that there seems to be a regular stream of envelopes taken daily by a maid from the chief chancery clerk's house to a mystery courier who waits in the gardens of Yeominster Square. He had the man watched, and found that he reads the contents, makes notes on them, and forwards them somewhere by normal mail. Jimmy said that his man was not able to intercept these envelopes, but that there might be some circumstances under which a senior person could do this. Is that correct, Adrian? And if so, would you be willing to let Jimmy Manley know who he should approach?"

"I'm sure something can be done, Alex – leave it with me and I'll take advice – first from Howard Anderson, even though it seems to fall outside diplomatic jurisdiction."

Alex and Melpomene took their leave, thanking Adrian Fitz-Hugh warmly for his help, collected their car from the yard and headed back to the flat, where Caroline informed them that Marjorie had said that they had received a number of calls – from Jimmy, Walter Huskisson and even Janice, saying that Sister Boniface had said she was allowed now to call Crabbe and Crabbe, for a good reason, and would be allowed to receive calls from them as well.

Mel said, "I will reply to that one first – it worries me a bit. Have you got the school number in your book, Alex?"

After a certain amount of conversation with the person who answered the telephone, including a rather haughty statement from her that the girls were now at dinner, Mel heard Janice's voice.

"Oh Melpomene!" she said, and there was a little quaver in her voice, "Mummy rang an hour ago from St Luke and said that Daddy had just left the island on a banana boat for England, leaving very little explanation and hardly even saying goodbye. She is rather upset, of course, and so am I, now! What can be going on, Mel?"

"Try and bear up for a moment, Janice! We'll see what we can find out from this end – we now have a contact in the Foreign Office. I'll get back to you in the morning, as soon as I've found out anything. Talk to Sister Boniface, she understands now!"

Chapter 26

As she had promised. Mel rang the Foreign Office as soon as she got to the office after breakfast. She asked for Mr Howard Anderson, and was passed from one secretary to the next until she was speaking to a woman who identified herself as *Sir* Howard's personal assistant. "What is the subject of your enquiry, Madam, since it is possible that I may be able to help you without bothering him?"

"Please tell *Sir* Howard that I was given his name by *Sir* Adrian Fitz-Hugh, Deputy Commissioner of the Metropolitan Police Force, and that my enquiry is of a highly confidential nature. I am the *Honourable* Mrs Melpomene Henrietta Crabbe, née Musgrave.

When Anderson came on the line, he said, "You are very prompt, Mrs Crabbe – Adrian Fitz-Hugh was only telling me about your case ten minutes ago! How can I help?"

"Since my husband, Alex, and I were talking to Adrian yesterday, I have had a rather distressed call from Janice Sharpe, the daughter of the diplomat in question, the military attaché in the British Embassy in St Luke, saying that her mother had just telephoned to tell her that her father had left on a banana boat for England with very little explanation!"

"First, I should reassure you that the choice of a banana boat is not particularly significant. There are, of course, regular services by passenger lines, such as Cunard and the Holland America Line, between Caribbean ports and this country but their schedules are sometimes inconvenient, while the banana trade is much more frequent during the growing season. Secondly, I have been talking to the Chief of Protocol at our Embassy in Port Sylvestre, who, like you, has had misgivings about Colonel Sharpe. He told me that military attachés are always problematic, because secrecy is an essential element of their work, but Sharpe has been taking this rather too far. Recently, he has been disappearing from his office for days at a time – and when the Chief button-holed him about the last occasion, when he had been out of touch for nearly a week, he told him quite rudely that it was a matter between himself and the senior intelligence director in Whitehall, and that he must ask the Ambassador about it if he wanted to know more."

"So," asked Melpomene, "is there such an official in the Foreign Office, or was he trying something on? And surely the Ambassador has ultimate authority over his staff, doesn't he?"

"Well, it is not as clear-cut as all that, Mrs Crabbe, each of the senior officers of the Embassy does report to the Ambassador, of course, but they are, at the same time, responsible to a variety of Government departments. For example, Walter Huskisson, who I believe you know, is a commercial attaché, so he works closely with the Board of Trade, while comptrollers take orders from Treasury, more or less directly, since it is acknowledged that an Ambassador cannot possibly be *au fait* with every aspect of his team's duties – especially those who owe their appointment not to years of dedicated work in the Civil Service, but to the favour of the incumbent Prime Minister, say, or even of the Palace – I mention no names! And, to add to the complexity, there are also links between those departments and we in the Foreign Office."

"So, what can I tell poor Janice, to comfort her?" asked Melpomene, "Is her father heading for the high jump, or what?"

"I suggest you say this, Melpomene, if I may call you that. First that it will take two or even three weeks for her father to reach England, depending on the route this particular vessel is taking, and what intermediate ports she calls at. I can find out more precisely for you, given a day or two. Second, there is no real evidence to suppose that Sharpe is in the sort of serious trouble which would lead to his dismissal from the Diplomatic Service or indeed to criminal charges. It is possible that he has simply had his fill of the job and wants out. Tell Janice that I will make further enquiries, but that I am not worried at this stage and that she should just be patient. Encourage her to talk to her mother on the telephone – I will speak to Mrs Sharpe myself – later today, if I can reach her – for her sake and for mine."

Melpomene thanked Howard and rang off, immediately asking Marjorie to call Hillyard House School for her. Again she reached a rather snooty teacher, who said that the girls had only just gone to their classes, and she was reluctant to disrupt them. "I quite understand!" said Melpomene, "So perhaps you would be so kind as to pass her a message for me. It is rather important, so I will dictate it to you and have you read it back to me. My name is Melpomene Crabbe, I am calling from my agency, and the message is that I have been in communication with a senior official of the Foreign Office, who wishes to assure Janice Sharpe that she should have no immediate worries about her father, who is not expected to reach England for at least two weeks, maybe more, and that the gentleman at the Foreign Office is pursuing his enquiries and will let this agency and Janice have more information as soon as it comes to hand. Have you got all that down – please read it back – yes, you have done well, thank you. Now will you indulge me a little more and share this conversation with Sister Boniface? Thanks for your help."

Mel rang off, shaking her head, exclaiming "Teachers!" and seizing the cup of Lapsang Souchong and the jam tart that Winnie had decided she would need immediately.

Marjorie said, "Mel, I've got Jimmy on the other line – I told him you would soon be free!"

Jimmy said to her, "I've been talking to Deputy Commissioner Fitz-Hugh and he has told me the necessary steps we must take without delay, so please get Alex to drive you to Mile End Road as quickly as poss. I trust you're both packing iron all the time? Good. See you in a few minutes, I hope."

On the way there, Mel and Alex speculated about what was going on. "Maybe he is has an update on Reg Withers, or something on Cedric Douglas," said Alex, to which Mel answered, "Then why did he say nothing on the telephone?"

They parked the Riley in the yard at the station and went straight to the CI department, only to be met inside by Cec Thompson who said, "As an Inspector, Jimmy now rates his own office – but he still comes and drinks tea with us all the time! It's just along the hall to the right."

Indeed, they saw the door, with a newly-emblazoned sign, "Detective-Inspector James Manley, Officer I/C Criminal Investigation." Inside Jimmy was talking to a woman in civilian clothes, who he introduced as "My personal assistant, Detective-Constable Jennifer Sweet – but of course, you've met her before, she took shorthand notes for us on the Pilkington case. She will take you to the policewoman's rest-room, Melpomene and explain."

She led Mel to a room on the second floor with a daybed and some chairs, and said, "Take off all your clothes except your undies! Stockings off, too! You can put them all on the bed."

Chapter 27

Melpomene was slightly startled by this request, then shrugged and complied. When she was standing there just in her camiknickers, Jennifer handed her a towelling bathrobe and said, "Please take a seat in the bathroom, through that door there, and I'll see whether Lucy Stafford is ready for you. I won't keep you in the dark any longer, she is going to attend to your hair – she is an experienced hairdresser from a local salon and if you agree she is going to dye your beautiful blonde curls brown and straighten them out! When the emergency is over, your hair can be brought back to its present state. After she has finished and dried your hair, I shall bring in a small range of different-sized uniforms and help you dress up as a policewoman! What do you say to that?"

Melpomene laughed, saying, "I'm always ready for something new! Will I be able to arrest wrong-doers, too?"

"In fact," said Jennifer, "that's not as much of a silly question as you may have thought! You are going to be sworn in as a Special Constable, so that within the London area you will have the same powers as other police, such as myself!"

The hair business took quite a while, and Lucy the hairdresser explained that the dye she was using was not particularly permanent, but said, "You don't have to worry about it running down your face, though, and if you want to go back to your lovely golden blonde it'll take several applications of our special bleach, which is not peroxide – if you're not careful with that you can finish up with pure white hair! Trust me, madam, I've done this before!"

"What about the curls?" asked Mel. "That's no problem, either," said Lucy, "we use the same solutions as for a normal perm – we just don't put curlers in, but tie the hair up in straight bunches. You won't know yourself in an hour!"

"Good!" said Mel, "That's the whole point!"

As promised, when Melpomene eventually summoned up the courage to look at herself in the mirror, she could hardly believe her eyes, congratulating and thanking Lucy, who gathered up her equipment and left, smiling.

"Now for the uniform!" said Jennifer, "I noticed you were wearing your silk stockings rolled, but that won't be enough for these heavy black woollen jobs – you'll need a suspender belt like this to keep them up."

Mel tried on a full, navy blue woollen skirt, reaching to her calves, and a woollen tunic which buttoned right up to the neck, pulled in at the waist with a wide leather belt. "I wear a cotton shirt under the tunic, when I'm in uniform," said Jennifer, "the wool can get awfully itchy, especially in warm weather." Topping it all off was a round felt hat with a wide brim, and Mel found a pair of ankle boots that fitted her well out of the selection that Jennifer had brought.

"You'll have to polish all those buttons, and your belt and boots from time to time, otherwise you'll get testy remarks from your Sergeant on morning parade – but maybe you will not be made to endure such pleasures! And you've got a handy chain there for your whistle. By the way, the side pockets in the skirt of your tunic will take your little Beretta quite easily – remember to keep the flap unbuttoned for a quick draw!"

There was a brief ceremony, conducted by the officer in charge of the station, Superintendent Collins, in which she was sworn in as a Special Constable, and issued with a copy of Police Regulations, a truncheon, a whistle and a notebook and indelible pencil, after which Jennifer said, "Now let's see if you will pass muster with Jimmy and your husband! Or should I say your ex-husband, now you are now Woman Police Constable Henrietta Musgrave, warrant card number 8661!" and took her back to the CI office.

Jimmy and Alex in fact were suitably impressed – Alex even said that it would take a while before he could be comfortable with her in intimate circumstances!

Melpomene, or Henrietta, finally was unable to restrain herself any longer and exclaimed, "This is all very well, and I must thank you, Jimmy, for organizing it for me, but what is puzzling me is what I'm supposed to do now – supervise a pedestrian crossing at a school, escort fallen women to a shelter, or arrest shop-lifters in Woolworth's – or what?"

"I have a number of assignments for you, none as trivial as those!" said Jimmy, "You have been delegated to my section for the time being. Let's all have a cup of tea and a rock-cake or something in celebration, and then I can explain. I got Lapsang

Souchong in specially for my new staff member! Now stop playing with your truncheon, WPC Musgrave and pay attention!"

When they were all sitting comfortably and enjoying their refreshments, Jimmy pinned a large sheet of paper on the bulletin-board with a numbered list of tasks on it.

"Number 1." he said, "This will be a good test of your disguise, for a start. Tomorrow morning at 10.30, when the military attaché, Brigadier Douglas, should be safely at work, you should present yourself at his house, say who you are, and ask to see Mrs Douglas, saying that a complaint has been received. There is no need to be more specific until you are presented to her. If she agrees to see you, ask if you can talk to her privately and then tell her that a housemaid from one of the other Embassy houses called at your police station in a distressed state and complained that Brigadier Douglas, mentioning him by name, had made inappropriate advances. Again, there is no need to be specific at first – play it by ear according to her reactions. Make notes in your book, thank her for whatever she has told you, and take your leave politely. It really doesn't matter what she says, the primary object of the exercise is to disconcert Douglas, not to get information."

Melpomene thought very hard for a few moments and said, "You leave it up to me how I play this? What if she tells me something that might be valuable to us – should I pursue it?"

"By all means, WPC Musgrave, but stay in character whatever you do – don't reveal anything that a policewoman wouldn't know, including the fact that Douglas is the military attaché."

Melpomene nodded and made a note in her book.

Jimmy continued, "Now, Task No 2. Again this involves a visit to a house in Yeominster Square, but this time in the evening, because we want to catch Elizabeth O'Connor at home. Again, say that you are following up a complaint. If she agrees to see you, ask that it be in private, and then say that a gentleman had reported that he had approached the police because he had had no satisfactory answer from the newspaper in which there had been published a libellous article. Here is a cutting of the article, it begins, *'From the desk of Elizabeth O'Connor, diplomatic reporter. There is turmoil at the St Luke Embassy in Yeominster Square, following the arrest of an officer of the Embassy on currency charges…'* This is an entirely bogus article, confected by us!"

Chapter 28

Jimmy Manley went on, "There are at least three more tasks that I have in mind for you Melpomene – I mean Henrietta – but let's save them up until we see how successful the first two turn out. We must also decide what you are to do when you are not on duty. As far as I know, the villains in this case haven't yet found out about Crabbe and Crabbe – I presume you didn't talk about being detectives during your socializing with Embassy staff, so that only trusted people, like Walter Huskisson and Desmond McPhail, are in on the plot. Let's keep it that way, and we don't need to mention where your flat is either. One thing we realise that they do know about now is your Riley car – the famous instructions letter mentioned the make and the fact it is a tourer – so, Henrietta, you had better not drive it while you are in your police-woman's outfit!"

"I've been thinking a bit, Jimmy," said Melpomene, "I can easily revert to my true identity by simply wearing a cloche hat, or a head-scarf, anything that will cover my hair, and donning one of my normal outfits. But that depends on how our friend Reg Withers is going – any news on him, Jimmy?"

"Yes, yes! I was going to tell you all about him, but I got all distracted about the disguise! He has been discharged from the closed ward at the hospital and is now in custody in the holding cells at Pentonville. A specialist interrogator and I have had two sessions with him so far, with his solicitor present, which is a bit of a nuisance, because we have to assume that this man, though a solicitor in good standing with the Law Society – of course we checked – is less than pure and will promptly pass on anything he learns from us to the gang or whatever organization it is that is behind all this. The consequence is that we have to phrase our questions quite carefully. But the interrogator, Chief Inspector Clive Barrett, from CID headquarters at the Yard, seems very clever to me and has already extracted a number of juicy items. One that will specially interest you, Mel and Alex, is that Reg Withers boasted that he was in Douglas' regiment, the Rutland Light Infantry, for a while, in between spells in the pokey. This prompted me to check on Brigadier Douglas' military record with an old mate of mine in the Ministry of Defence, and he told me that the rumour at the time that he left the service, some five years ago, just after the Armistice, was that he got out just ahead of an investigation into rumours of manipulation of regimental funds. Nothing was proved, so Douglas remains clean – otherwise, of course, he could never have got into the diplomatic service!"

"I'm not at all surprised!" said Mel, "All the time I was talking to him at the Huskissons' silver wedding, I was thinking that I wouldn't buy a second-hand car from this man! But seriously, it sounds as though it would take more than being told that the police have been making enquiries to ruffle him, if that's the point in me going to his house – what do you think, Jimmy?"

"You're right, Mel," said Jimmy, "but my idea was simply to apply a little pressure – you told me before that he very quickly raised his hackles when you asked about his relations with the police and the customs service, didn't he?"

"That's right, he shifted into another gear, so I changed the subject! So a few enquiries from a humble policewoman will be enough to niggle him, you think? But anyway I'll still see what I can get out of Mrs Douglas. Another thought – I had better do sommat abaht me accent wouldn't you say, wivaht goin' over the top! Not that the policemen and women that I've spoken to recently have been out-and-out cockneys, but maybe my own accent occasionally gets a bit 'cut-glass' – what do you say, Jimmy, me old cock-sparrer?"

"More important than accent is vocabulary and expressive style, I would think," put in Alex, "especially when you move on to talking to Elizabeth O'Connor – as a writer she might be more sensitive to language than the others you'll be speaking to. Don't know much about Mrs Douglas, she was a bit out of it at the restaurant."

"Well, enough talking about it!" said Jimmy Manley, "You'd better go home by Tube, Mel, given what we said about your car – have you got change for the ticket? The common belief that the police travel free on public transport is just not true, I'm sorry to have to tell you – it only applies when you are on duty!"

It was quite late in the afternoon when Melpomene arrived at the flat, and she supposed that Alex has already got home, so she hoped he hadn't said anything to Caroline or Mrs Mountain about her transformation.

She rang the front-door bell instead of using her key – in any case it was with her clothes and other things in one of the carrier-bags that Cec Thomson had found for her – she had fortunately thought to transfer her change to her pocket to pay for her Underground ticket.

Caroline opened the door, and when she saw a policewoman standing there let out a cry, "What's happened, is Mrs Crabbe all right?"

Melpomene was immediately sorry, realising that the sudden appearance of an officer on the doorstep frequently presaged bad news of one sort or another, so she spoke in her natural voice, "It's all right, Caroline, my dear, it's only Mel! I'm dressed like this as a disguise!" and she hugged her.

Recovering, Caroline was able to force a laugh, saying, "It's your best disguise yet, Mel – much more convincing than the old flower-seller or the gas inspector! Come in and let me have a good look at you! Alex just telephoned from the office, but he didn't say anything – I suppose you put him up to it!"

"My goodness, they've done a good job on your hair! Will you ever be able to get it back to its proper colour and style?"

"I sincerely hope so, Caroline, otherwise I'll sue the Metropolitan Police for a huge amount! The hairdresser who did it told me that the colour and the curls can be brought back as soon as all this unpleasantness is over. By the way, I'm now WPC Henrietta Musgrave, No. 8661 – Melpomene Crabbe is away on holidays somewhere inaccessible if anyone asks for her! You said Alex phoned – what was it about? Anything for me?"

"He could still be there, try calling him, Mel – I mean Henrietta!"

Alex answered straight away, as though he had been standing by the telephone, "Mel – or whoever you are at the moment – I just heard from Walter Huskisson. He was in a dreadful panicky state and hardly coherent, but he asked if one or both of us could go to his place straight away. How long would it take you to change back into civvies and cover your hair? I'll come and pick you up straight away and we can drive there and park just round the corner so that the Riley can't be spotted outside his house. I'll wait outside, so come down as soon as you're ready. Bring your pistol – I'm carrying mine now!"

Chapter 29

As they arrived on foot at the Huskissons' house, having left the car out of sight, they could see Walter standing on the steps, looking anxiously one way and the other. When he spotted Mel and Alex, he came down to meet them, saying, "Thank goodness you are here – I didn't want to call the police before I checked with you! Come inside and I'll tell you all about it – some of my neighbours have a tendency to peer out from behind their lace curtains!"

Once inside, Mel could see that he was in a highly agitated state, so she took his elbow and led him to sit next to her on a settee in the sitting-room.

"Now take a deep breath, Walter, and tell us what has happened."

"Marie-Colette has disappeared!" he wailed, "Maybe an hour ago, but I'm not completely sure, because I was busy doing the household accounts at the time. We gave the staff the evening off, and Marie-Colette was in the kitchen – at the back of this floor – preparing our evening meal – onion soup, I think, and a mixed bean casserole. I heard the front door bell ring and I was about to go down – my office is on the first floor – when I heard voices in the hall, so I assumed that Marie-Colette was dealing with the visitor. Then I heard the door slam, so I went to the head of the stairs and called out. There was no answer, so I rushed down, went out of the front door and looked up and down the square. I was just in time to see the rear light of a car or taxi disappearing towards the road that leads from the square to the north. I was beside myself as you can imagine – I looked everywhere in the house, but she had gone!"

"Did you think of telephoning the police?" asked Alex.

"Yes, but when I got to the telephone I thought I had better try you first – I know how pedestrian police enquiries can sometimes be! And somehow I thought this must be to do with whoever is responsible for the questionable activities around the Embassy!"

At this point, they heard the front door bell ring. Walter jumped up and ran to open it, closely followed by Alex, who had his hand on the butt of his pistol in its shoulder-holster.

On the doorstep stood a small, scruffy boy, holding an envelope, who said, "I'm s'posed to give this to Mr Hutchinson, and the bloke said then I'd get another shillin' to go with the one he give me!"

Walter seized the envelope, and Alex grasped the kid by the arm and brought him inside, saying, "I'll give you your shilling, but only if you answer some questions!"

He plonked him down on a chair in the hallway and said, "Who gave you this letter?" but before the boy could answer, Walter had ripped open the envelope and read the single sheet of paper inside, almost bursting into tears. Melpomene led him gently back into the sitting-room, sat him down and took the letter, which read *'If you want your wife back in one piece, do not talk to the police – if we find out you have done this you will see her next at her funeral, if at all! We are keeping observation on you night and day! We will inform you very soon of the amount of the reward we are asking and the means by which you are to convey it to us! Do nothing till you hear from us – the code word is "BLACKBEARD" – wait for our next message! Please give the bearer of this note a shilling for his trouble!'*

Mel put her arm round Walter's shoulders – by this time he was sobbing. In the hallway, Alex was saying, "Now, young feller-me-lad, who was it gave you this letter, and how did it happen?"

"Well mister, it was like this!" the kid was starting to enjoy the drama of the situation! "I had just took my takings from selling newspapers back to Mr Goodman at the newsagents' and this bloke comes up and says 'Want to earn a quick bob?' I says, 'Yus, I wouldn't mind!' and he says, 'You know Yeominster Square?' I says, 'O'course, it's on'y a step from 'ere!' and he gives me the letter, saying 'Take this to Mr Hutchinson at Number 12 and give it to him, not to his maid or nobody else. Here's a shillin' and Mr Hutchinson will give you another!' So I took it and brung it 'ere – will you give me me shillin'?"

"Not just yet, I want you to tell me what he was like, this man."

"He was big – taller'n you and more hefty, like. He'd a cap pulled down over his forrid, and he was wearin' a greasy mac. His boots looked like they could do with some polish. I know boots, because I sometimes do boot-blackin' at 'otels when they need somebody extra. And he 'ad string round the knees of 'is trousies – dunno what for!"

"Very good, sonny – here's your shilling and you can have another one if you'll tell me your name and where I can find you again!" said Alex.

"That's easy!" said the boy, "Me name's Colin Stammers, and I always sells me papers outside the Red Lion of an evening, starting about six o'clock until they're all gone, usually by about eight or 'alf past. Oh, thanks, guv'nor!" and he was gone!

Alex went into the sitting-room, where Walter had calmed down a little, "Here is the letter," Mel said, "stay with Walter, and I'll go and see if I can make us all cups of tea – is tea all right, Walter?"

"If its not too much trouble, I would like chamomile – it seems to calm me down, and I could do with that – I'm sorry I'm making such a fuss, but I'm worried stiff!"

"Of course," said Mel, "we fully understand – but we'll be onto it as soon as we can. The second message will tell us more!"

She disappeared toward the kitchen and soon came back with a tray of tea things and some biscuits. "I turned off the gas under the bean casserole!" she said, "It hadn't started to burn, but it would have before very long! I hope I made the chamomile the way you like it, Walter – I assume you don't take it with milk or sugar?"

"Thank you so much, Melpomene!" Walter said, taking a sip "That's excellent! What I'm wondering is what we should do next – should we really obey instructions and not contact the police?"

Said Alex, "Kidnappers warn about not contacting the police ninety-nine times out of hundred, but what they don't realise is that there are ways of doing this very cautiously so that nobody outside finds out. And it helps if you know someone in the force, too. May I use your telephone, Walter? And if you trust us, we'll try talking to Detective-Inspector Jimmy Manley, who you already know. I should have his home number in my little notebook."

Jimmy was at home and listened intently to the whole story. When Alex had finished, he said, "As I might have expected, you two have done the right things – good work with the paper-boy! Next we wait for the promised second message – I assume you are staying with Walter for the moment? I won't come there, they are likely to be watching, as they threatened!"

Chapter 30

Melpomene said, "I don't know about you two, but I'm getting rather hungry – if it's all right with you, Walter, why don't we make sure that Marie-Colette's bean casserole doesn't go to waste while we're waiting for these crooks to contact you?"

"You're quite right, Mel," said Walter, "and did you check the onion soup, too? Let's go and eat something in the kitchen, otherwise we'll go spare with the waiting."

They were soon enjoying the soup, which only had to be heated up a little, and the casserole, which was delicious, with some Hovis bread. All had their ears cocked for the front door bell – they had left the kitchen door open – but they almost missed the sound of the letter-flap on the door being opened.

Alex ran to the door, whipped it open and dashed out, but he was too late to see who it might have been. He ran out to the front gate and looked up and down, but still saw nothing, so he went back inside. Walter had opened a second envelope and read it out.

"It seems to be in the same handwriting as the first one, and says, *'If you desire to see your wife in one piece again, place £10,000 in used one-pound notes – NOT fivers, in a biscuit tin, wrap it up neatly in brown paper and string, and stand underneath the clock at Liverpool Street Station at 5 o'clock the day after tomorrow until someone comes up and says the password. Give it to this person and stand still – if you attempt to follow, or if we find that you have cheated on the money, we shall cut off one of your wife's ears and send it to you and the ransom will double!'* Oh, this is terrible – how can anyone be so wicked!" and he sank down on a chair and started weeping again.

Melpomene tried to comfort him, holding his hand and patting his back, but he raised his head and said through his tears, "All I can do is follow these instructions – I dare not do otherwise! And let me beseech you – please do not do anything that will upset them – they are obviously capable of what they are threatening! And what guarantee have we got that they will let Marie-Colette free even after I pay the ransom?"

Alex said, "Fortunately, Walter, we have plenty of time to think. I have had a couple of thoughts which might be useful.

First of all, the writing and language are of a quality that would not be expected of an uneducated person – there are no spelling mistakes or grammatical errors and the handwriting is neat and appears to have been written with a fountain-pen. Secondly, I suspect that the second letter was put through your door by somebody local – possibly living only a few doors away – there was no time for anything else. And taking this a bit further, you saw a car or taxi disappearing after Marie-Colette was taken, but that doesn't necessarily mean that she was actually in that car – she may just have been bundled into a house nearby! Who are your immediate neighbours, Walter?"

"Well, this side of the square are the even numbers – the more senior officials live this side – we are No. 12, and we have what originally were Numbers 14 to 16 to our right, these days they have become the Chancery, the Embassy main building, with, in a new extension behind, the official apartments of the Ambassador, Chevalier de Chapelle and Madame de Chapelle, the head of Chancery, M Lavalier, the Chief of Protocol, M du Pont, and the Comptroller, Mr Sidmouth, and then we get back to detached houses, starting with No. 18 – the McPhails, that you have already visited, and then No. 20 – that's Brigadier and Mrs Douglas. Elizabeth O'Connor lives at No. 8, two doors down on our left. Over the other side of the square the houses are a bit smaller, and most of the junior professional staff live there – the secretaries, mail clerks, telephone operators and so on mostly live elsewhere and have to commute daily."

"You didn't mention No. 10," said Alex, "unless I missed it – who lives there?"

"That's a special case," replied Walter, "it's a house that has no connection with the embassy at all! I'm told that when the embassy was being planned, most of the houses in the square were purchased at attractive prices for the time, so the owners were only too happy to accept what they were offered. But there were a few exceptions, No. 10 being one. The owners were elderly spinster sisters who had lived in the house all their lives and wished to stay there until they died – and one indeed got her wish and succumbed to the Spanish flu epidemic in 1919. Her sister survived, but was forced to take in lodgers to maintain her comfortable lifestyle. Most of what we know of her is through our housemaid, Muriel, who is on good terms with her opposite number next door – her name is Peggy, I think. The old lady herself is rarely seen, and we have never spoken to her. Occasionally we see one of her lodgers taking the sun in the garden, or leaving the house to go somewhere, but we have never spoken to any of them, either – at least, I haven't, maybe Marie-Colette has – oh dear, I had forgotten her for a moment!"

He sat down and looked upset again, so Alex said, in a business-like tone, "Why I asked about your neighbours, Walter, is because I'm beginning to think that Marie-Colette might not have been in that taxi or car you saw leaving the square, but hidden next door! And that would explain how we missed the person who put the second message through the front door letter-slot – what if these villains are lodging at No. 10!"

"We can hardly ring the bell and ask if they have any hostages!" said Melpomene, "But there may be other ways of having a peep inside – and, another thing, Elizabeth O'Connor ought not to be overlooked either – she's quite close and we know she can be dishonest!"

"Walter," said Alex, "we obviously can't do anything more tonight – we've received the ransom note proper, and we can't act on it until the day after tomorrow. I suppose they wanted to give you time to raise the money, but the delay works in our favour, because we can take the time to plan our next activities. We'll ask Jimmy Manley if he knows of any ransom experts at the Yard – I'll be surprised if there aren't. And, we assure you, Walter, that we won't do anything precipitate – in fact we'll check with you before we move at all!"

"Will you be alright here on your own?" asked Melpomene, "You'd be quite welcome to come home with us, you know."

"Thanks for the thought, Mel!" said Walter, "But I couldn't bear to go anywhere else, in case these crooks try to get in touch again. It's not as though I'll be alone, Muriel and our housekeeper, Mrs Beeton – yes, really! – both live in, and they should be back from the pictures soon – and our daily arrives soon after eight in the morning."

"Well, don't hesitate to ring us, whatever the time, and however trivial you might think it is, we shall be in the flat until after breakfast, and then we'll go to the office. There will be someone to take calls at both places all the time if you miss us in transit, so go ahead if you feel you'd like to talk."

Chapter 31

Mel and Alex had hardly arrived home, when Walter Huskisson took them at their word and called.

"I hope that this is not a waste of your time!" he said, "But our housemaid, Muriel Dodds, had something she thought was strange to report to me as soon as she and Mrs Beeton arrived back from the pictures. I interrupted her, of course, to tell them about Marie-Colette – they were both appalled, as you would think. Muriel even broke down and cried, and took a while to be consoled by me and Hettie Beeton. But after we had all had a cup of something and talked about what could be done – none of us had anything sensible to suggest – I asked Muriel what she was going to tell me when she arrived."

He paused for a moment, and Melpomene, who had taken the call, said, "Take your time, Walter, Alex is listening too."

"This could be valuable information, but it's hard to know! What she told me was that, as they opened the front gate to come in, they heard a cat miaowing. Muriel called out 'Mopsy, Mopsy', thinking it might be Marie-Colette's cat of that name, and, sure enough, he came up to her and rubbed against her legs, as he always does, but what interested Muriel was that he came from the next-door front garden, jumping the wall. That's No 10, that I told you about before!"

"Is it usual for him to be out at night?" asked Mel, "It's quite late – does he come back to sleep in the house?"

"He's a ginger tom, and Marie-Colette always says that it's normal for a tom to range quite widely. There's a cat-flap in the kitchen door and he comes and goes as he pleases, but he always seeks her out in the evenings and comes to sit on her lap while she's reading or listening to the wireless, or talking to me. Last night he was obviously looking for her – he went round and round, from her bedroom to the kitchen, the dining-room and the sitting-room, miaowing all the time. He's finally settled down in her chair in the sitting-room, but every time someone moves, he raises his head and looks. Poor Mopsy – he's missing Marie-Colette as much as I am!"

"It's too late to do anything tonight, of course, Walter, but all this has given me some ideas I'd like to follow up – would it be alright with you if I come over first thing tomorrow? When do you have to go to work?"

"Don't worry about that, Melpomene, I shall let them know the situation and just stay here."

"No, Walter, please don't tell anyone at the Embassy what has happened – we still don't know who to trust – just say you are sick or something! I'll see you about half-past eight – but I need to discuss things with Alex first, so it could be later!"

Alex had been listening to this conversation and thinking what was best to do. He said to Mel, "Since Walter was specifically warned not to call the police, you had better not go there as a policewoman – but that still leaves two identities for you to call on! If you cover your hair with a scarf or cloche hat you revert to being Melpomene Crabbe – and the forces of evil are already aware that you and I know Walter and Marie-Colette socially, since some of them were undoubtedly present at the silver wedding party! So we can appear at the Huskissons' place without causing further alarm, although we shall certainly be watched. Alternatively, if you reveal the new colour and style of your hair and wear a different outfit from your usual ones, you can take on a third personality – but maybe you should change your face a little as well, to make a further distinction. How could you do that, Mel?"

"Let me think, Alex. I don't know if you notice this sort of thing, my dear, but I normally use a pale ivory face-powder, and when I put on lipstick – which isn't always – it's in a bright red 'cupid's bow', and then I use a little rose-coloured rouge. For eye makeup I stick to light brownish shades for my eyebrows, and darker brown for my lashes and eye-liner. What did you think I was doing in the bathroom every morning?"

"I didn't like to ask! So you can change these arrangements, can you?"

"I'll have to see whether I can borrow some stuff from Caroline for now – there's no time for me to go and buy it this morning – she, having black hair, goes in for a rather different look when she goes out – beige Rachel powder and much bolder around the eyes. I'll darken my eyebrows and use eye-shadow and mascara – and use a darker lipstick, too – that should create a whole new look. I'll wear a boring brown dress that I tried once and then didn't like. It's a bit longer that what's being worn now."

"Next we had better ring Jimmy and put him in the picture about Marie-Colette!" said Alex, "He may have some suggestions, too, and he can tell us whether there is a kidnap expert at the Yard."

Jimmy listened intently to the account that Alex gave, occasionally asking questions about details, and then said, "I agree it would be good to go to Walter's house this morning, and you are quite right not to confuse things by introducing PCW Musgrave yet – she has other work to do! There is no hurry to comply with their requests about the ransom money yet – tomorrow will be early enough to get it – have you asked Walter whether he will have any difficulty raising the £10,000? You are quite right about specialists at Scotland Yard who are used to dealing with kidnappers – I will get onto them as soon as I ring off. Play it by ear as you usually do, and let me know what happens. I still have a man across the gardens keeping watch with binoculars – but I doubt whether he was able to see anything last evening – I shall ask him all the same. I already called off the other watchers, which is a shame. Give me a call here if anything interesting happens!"

While this conversation was going on, Melpomene had been to see Caroline, and with her help was applying her new make-up in the bathroom. She combed her hair into a neat side parting and donned her boring brown dress, so when she emerged to show Alex, he showed a certain amount of shock!

"Very good, my darling!" he said, "This may be a back-handed compliment, but I would pass you in the street without a second glance – it must have been the blonde curls that attracted me in the first place! And your intellect, of course, but that is not immediately visible!"

"We mustn't be seen together while I'm like this, otherwise the spell might be broken." said Mel, "While I was dressing, I was looking at Caroline and this gave me the idea for another plan. Perhaps you could drop me where we parked last night – you could go for coffee or something and come the house after an hour. By that time, my ingenious plan will either have worked or not – we shall see!"

So after they had parked, Melpomene walked to the house, rang the bell and was met by a smart maid in a black dress with a white pinafore and collar. Mel looked at her and gave a satisfied nod.

Chapter 32

The maid greeted Melpomene and politely asked her business.

"I've come to talk to Mr Huskisson – it's about Madame Huskisson's disappearance – I'm a friend of both of them – you can let him know in a while that I've called, but I don't want to bother him too much – he is probably still very upset."

"Yes, madam, when I peeped in his bedroom a few minutes ago he was still fast asleep. He told Cook and me all about it last night – it's a terrible thing!"

"It's about all this that I want to talk to you, Muriel – it is Muriel isn't it? Good. I believe you are on friendly terms with Peggy, the maid from No. 10, so I wanted to take advantage of this to find out more about what is going on there. We – my husband Alex and I – believe that Madam Huskisson might be being held there against her will."

Muriel exclaimed, "Now you mention Mr Alex, I realize why you seem a bit familiar – I couldn't work it out before – are you wearing a wig?"

"Not exactly, Muriel – would you have recognized me if I hadn't mentioned Alex? – That's good. Now I want to disguise myself a little more so I can go next door and see what I can find out. I guess we are about the same size – will you lend me one of your uniforms for a while?"

Muriel was getting quite excited! She took Mel up to her room and helped her change into a maid's outfit – she was already wearing stockings and shoes that would pass.

"I'm going to tell your friend Peggy next door a few white lies – I won't cause any trouble for you, Muriel – will that be alright with you?"

"Oh, yes, madam, as long as it will help to get Madame Huskisson back to us!"

Muriel showed the new maid the door leading into the back garden, and pointed out a gate leading to the garden of No. 10.

"Mostly I just breeze into the kitchen next door, and at this time of day I often find Peggy preparing a breakfast tray for old Miss Cavanagh, the owner. If she's not there, I just make myself a cup of tea and wait – Peggy and I are on very friendly terms! Miss Cavanagh has her room on the ground floor now, one up from the basement where the kitchen is – she has trouble with the stairs since she walks with a stick, but she has all that she needs on that floor. The lodgers I think are on the upper floors, but I never have much to do with them, of course. Peggy will tell you how many there are of them at present, the number changes from time to time, she tells me."

Melpomene found her way to the kitchen door of the next house and went in, seeing a maid putting a pot of marmalade, some toast and two boiled eggs on a tray. She was waiting for the kettle to boil and had a teapot ready. She looked up and saw Mel and a puzzled expression formed on her face, but before she had a chance to speak, Mel said, "Hello, Peggy, isn't it? Muriel next door said I would find you in the kitchen. Please take your tray to Miss Cavanagh while the tea is still hot, and then I'll explain to you what I'm doing here!"

Peggy was about to say something, but then shrugged and took the tray out. After a few minutes, she reappeared, and said, "This is all very strange – who are you and what are you doing here? Is Muriel alright?"

Melpomene said, "I may be dressed like a maid, but my name is Henrietta Musgrave and I'm really a female police detective – here is my warrant card! I'm here because we are trying to find Madame Huskisson from next door, who we think has been kidnapped! She vanished early last evening, so we are making a thorough search of the neighbourhood. I'm dressed this way so as not to frighten off any of the guilty parties we might come across. Muriel has told us you have lodgers here – can you tell me about them, please? How many are there in the house right now?"

"I like the Huskissons very much, so I'll do what I can to help," said Peggy, "the two lodgers we have at present are very unpleasant – always throwing their weight around. We haven't got a full-time cook, now there's only me and Miss Cavanagh and her nurse, Sister Wallace, who has the room next to hers, so she can be called any time she is needed. The cook, Mrs Sisley, comes in in the afternoons to prepare dinner for the household, and I make breakfast, first for me and the nurse, and then for Miss Cavanagh, and lunch for all three of us, too, while those men mainly eat out. Yesterday, for a change, they wanted a full dinner, so I had to go and do the shopping once Mrs Sisley had decided what to cook. We had tomato soup and lamb chops and veges, followed by rice pudding with sultanas in it – it was very nice, but the lodgers did nothing but complain – but I noticed they ate a lot, all the same!"

"Where do you all eat, Peggy, in the dining-room, or what?" asked Mel.

"Oh no, Miss Cavanagh has hers in her room, with Sister Wallace – and Mrs Sisley and I eat here, in the kitchen. The lodgers have theirs in their private sitting-room on the second floor near their bedrooms. They're both in today."

"Are there any other rooms in regular occupation? I suppose you have a room higher up, as is usual for live-in staff."

"I did a while ago, but I asked if I could sleep down here – I have a little room next to this kitchen. I was on the top floor before, but I didn't like being on my own up there, especially with strange men around. So my old room is out of use now."

"I'm going to ask you something that may sound strange, Peggy – do you clean the inside of the windows yourself, or do you have a window-cleaner?"

"Yes, a man comes round every few weeks with his ladder and buckets to do them, but only for the outsides – so I do the insides, but I haven't done them recently – why do you ask, Henrietta?"

"Because I'm going to go up and do them for you, my dear! Please find me a bucket, or whatever you use, and the rags and Windolene and polishing cloths, and I'll go up to the top floor and work my way downwards. You are in the know about why I'm here, Peggy, so you may not find it difficult to guess that this is simply a ruse, so I can go and poke about!"

"Oh, Henrietta, please be careful – those lodgers are not nice people at all! If they suspect that you're not what you seem, they could get rough! If they've really taken Madame Huskisson prisoner, what's to stop them grabbing you, too!"

"Thanks for your concern, Peggy, but I have a little friend with me!" and she gave her a peep at the pistol she had in her apron pocket.

"It's possible that Muriel will send my husband round if he arrives before I've finished, so if he asks could you let him know what I'm up to, please?"

Chapter 33

Melpomene took the window-cleaning paraphernalia and headed for the stairs, while Peggy reminded her on what floors were the rooms in question. She listened at two of the smaller rooms on the ground floor, and heard a quiet conversation between two female voices. She nodded and thought, "Miss Cavanagh and the nurse."

She did not venture along the next landing, but could hear at least two men talking loudly and laughing. There was a strong smell of cigarette smoke, and there were several empty beer bottles lined up outside one of the doors. She pressed on, up the stairs. The wainscot and rich wallpapers of the ground and second floors gave way up here to cream-painted walls like those in the basement. There were three doors at this level.

Melpomene put her equipment down by the window at what must have been the street end of the landing, and cautiously turned the knob of the nearest door, finding that it was unlocked. Peering inside, she could see that it was a box-room, filled with a miscellany of discarded household items, cane-bottomed chairs, fire-screens, whatnots and the like. She softly closed the door and tried the next. This room was almost empty except for a roll of carpet.

The last room on the floor she found was locked. She was about to tap on it, but heard footsteps on the stairs, so she quietly went and started to wipe down the window with a sponge and warm water. Then a male voice said, in an aggressive tone, "I thought you were told never to come up here? Oh, I don't know you, I took you for the maid Peggy!"

"Oh, sorry, sir!" said Mel, almost curtseying but stopping herself at the last moment, "I'm the new maid, what's come to take over for when Peggy goes on her holidays next week! I didn't know I wasn't s'posed to be on this floor. Should I finish the window now, while I'm here?"

The man scowled, but said, "Oh, I suppose so, but don't come up here again, this is private! I'll have a word with Peggy about it!"

Mel turned back to the window and took her time, wiping it off, applying the Windolene and polishing it. She could see that the man had lit a cigarette and was walking up and down impatiently. He was fairly short and bald, wearing a shabby suit and scuffed two-toned shoes. Mel muttered "Co-respondent shoes" to herself.

She gathered up her equipment and headed for the stairs. As she started to go down, she glanced back and could see that the man was unlocking the door, but she couldn't risk stopping and watching him.

On the next floor below, she went and cleaned the window on the street frontage, and then knocked on the next door. There was no answer, so she went in, finding it was a sitting room with a small dining table to one side and several chairs. There were newspapers on one of the chairs and piled on the floor. Mel went in and dutifully started cleaning the two windows, deliberately making a clatter with the bucket and singing "Sweet Georgia Brown" which was always being played on the wireless now.

This had the effect she desired, as a man – not the one she had just seen – came into the room and said, "What are you up to – when we want the windows cleaned we'll ask! Who are you, anyway?"

Mel fed him the same story she had told before, which satisfied him, so he left, saying, "Don't bother with the other rooms on this floor – the middle one doesn't have no windows, and the one next the stairs is our private bedroom!"

"Thank you, sir!" said Mel, "I'll go down and do the first floor now!"

As she headed for the stairs, the first man came along, and as Mel started going down, she heard him say to his companion, "She ain't looking too good, Stan, p'r'aps we ought to get the doctor to 'er!" His mate hushed him, saying "Watch yer mouth, Alf, d'you want to blow everything!"

At that, Mel ran all the way down to the kitchen and set the cleaning gear down. She was panting a bit, and Peggy said, "Are you alright, Henrietta?", to which she replied, "I think they've got Marie-Colette up there! No signs of Alex, yet?"

"Sit down and have a cup of tea, dear, I've just made a fresh pot – meanwhile I'll run next door and see if I can find out from Muriel where your husband has got to!"

102

Melpomene had only just finished her tea, when Alex and Peggy came back through the garden.

Mel explained what she had found out, saying, "I'm can't be absolutely certain, Alex, but I really have no doubt that Marie-Colette is locked up in a room on the top floor. But the two villains are alert now, so we have to take things very carefully. I didn't see any guns, but we know that this lot are fond of them – I still remember the feeling of a cold barrel on the back of my neck! Have you got your Luger with you, Alex? I've got my little Beretta in my pinny pocket!"

"Nevertheless, Mel, my dear, we shouldn't tackle this like a bull at a gate – we need to employ diversionary tactics. We could, of course, call on Jimmy Manley to bring in a bunch of police, but this would frighten off any other malefactors, especially those lurking within the embassy. Peggy, where is the telephone in this house – is there more than one? Do you know the names of these two – or at least the names they're going by at the moment?"

"The only telephone is on the first floor, near the front door. This the floor where Miss Cavanagh and the nurse's rooms are. And the men are called Mr Rowley and Mr Macnamara."

"Good, Peggy – you are being very helpful already – will you do another thing for us? Run next door and ask Muriel to call this telephone in ten minutes. It doesn't matter what she says, all we want the crooks to do is hear it ring – can they hear it from up there?"

"Oh, yes, they put in a specially loud bell, because Miss Cavanagh is a little hard of hearing."

"Then once it has rung and you've taken a pretend message, do you feel up to going up and telling them there is a call for Mr Rowley or Mr Macnamara?"

"Oh yes, I've taken calls for them before, from someone calling himself Bennett – they always jump to it when they hear that name!"

"Oh, excellent, Peggy, I'll kiss you later, when Me... Henrietta is not looking!"

She disappeared out of the garden door and returned in five minutes, giving the 'thumbs-up' signal. Then they heard the telephone ring on the next floor.

Chapter 34

Alex and Henrietta took Peggy up to the ground floor, and waited in what was apparently the disused dining-room, with the door open so that they had a view of the telephone, still ringing, while Alex told Peggy what was going to happen, "I'll just go and answer it, and tell Muriel what to do. When I've done that I'll let you know, and then you can go up to their room on the second floor to tell them that there is a call for Mr Rowley or Mr Macnamara – it doesn't matter who takes it, either or even both of them. Then, Henrietta and I will see what happens and deal with the situation, while you wait here, keeping out of sight!"

Alex picked up the telephone and spoke to Muriel, "This is Alex, Muriel. Hang on until you hear one of the crooks speak – when he does you can say, in an official-sounding voice, something like 'There is a call for you from Mr Bennett, please wait ...' and then just stop talking – whatever they say, just keep quiet, but don't hang up! Then, please tell Mr Huskisson what is going on and ask him to come over here with you and wait in the kitchen."

He put the telephone earpiece down, nodded to Peggy and she went up the stairs. Alex said to Henrietta, "I hope you're carrying your Beretta loaded and cocked? Take the safety off now – I'll do the same with my Luger. If only one comes, leave him to me, but cover me. If both of them arrive, that'll be a little more awkward – I'll take the one who answers the telephone, and leave the other to you. We'll keep out of sight here until we have to act!"

"If they go for their own guns, remember that Jimmy recommends a shot to the shoulder!

In the event, it was the tall one – not the one in co-respondent shoes – who picked up the telephone. He said. "Macnamara", listened and then waited. When nothing happened immediately, he shouted into the telephone, "Macnamara here, why don't you answer?" but, hearing nothing, threw the earpiece down, turned, and was confronted by Alex aiming his pistol at his chest and saying, "Hands on your head, quickly, before I plug you!" and then, as the man did so, "Now, keep your hands where they are and sit down with your back against the wall! Now, Hen, cover him while I go for the other one! If he tries anything, shoot him like you did that other guy! One bullet in each shoulder should do the trick!"

Macnamara watched Alex disappear towards the stairs, and then tried to sneak one of his hands down, but quickly replaced it when Henrietta raised her pistol a little and said "Come on, mister, just give me an excuse!"

As Alex started up the stairs, he saw the other man, Rowley, ahead of him, going up to the top floor. He followed him quietly and peered round the corner, to see that Rowley was unlocking a door and entering the room. Alex quickly followed him, and Luger held ready, stepped in.

The man was standing by a figure covered by blankets on the bed, saying, "Wake up, missus, you got to get up now!" but as he did so, Marie-Colette stepped out from behind a wardrobe and hit him on the head with a heavy china chamber-pot! He staggered but just managed to stay upright.

And then Alex shouted "Hold it, I've got you covered, put your hands on your head!" and levelled his pistol at his chest. The man complied, and Marie-Colette burst into nervous laughter!

"*Je suis si heureux de vous voir, M Alex!*" she said, "They must have given me a sedative in a glass of milk last night – I only woke half an hour ago, and I was extremely peeved that I had been treated so! I am not the sort of woman to take bad treatment meekly!"

"So I see!" said Alex, "Let us proceed." To Rowley he said, "Sit on the floor with your back against the wall and don't try anything, I'm getting peeved, too, and my temper is quite short!" and he covered the man.

"Now, Madame, are you steady on your feet? Please go down to the kitchen – Walter should be there very shortly."

"I will, Alex, but shouldn't I disarm this fellow first? I know that he carries a pistol in a shoulder holster! I will make sure not to get between your gun and him!" and she slipped her hand under his jacket and pulled out a revolver, "I'll take this with me, will I?"

"If you feel up to disarming the other one," said Alex, laughing, "Melpomene has him covered on the ground floor – see what she says! When this is all over, Marie-Colette, you might consider joining our agency!"

Then he motioned with his gun to Rowley, "Get to your feet, nice and slowly, and walk ahead of me down the stairs. Don't try anything, or even stumble, I have an itchy trigger finger, as they say in the pulp magazines!"

At the ground floor level, there was Henrietta, conducting Macnamara ahead of her in the same way, explaining, "Marie-Colette disarmed this one – what a woman!"

In the kitchen, they saw Walter and Marie-Colette embracing tearfully – but Walter immediately said "What should I do to help – up to now I've been just an observer!"

"Fine, you and Peggy can tie their hands behind them – have you got some strong clothes-line or something, Peggy? Just make sure not to obscure my line of sight or Henrietta's while you are doing it. And then, Walter, you can ring Jimmy Manley up – do you remember his number? I have it anyway – and ask him if he would kindly send a Black Maria and several burly policemen to No. 10 Yeominster Square to pick up some customers!"

Once the two were securely tied up, Alex sat them both down against the wall, not too close to each other, but close enough that he could cover them both with his Luger.

"Now, Peggy," said Henrietta, "how about cups of tea all round – if you have tisane, Walter and Marie-Colette would prefer it, I think – you wouldn't have any jam tarts or similar would you?"

"Let me see," said Peggy, "I have some fruit-cake and some Bourbon biscuits – how about those? Or I could make toast and even some omelettes, if anybody is getting really peckish!"

Then a woman in a white coat appeared at the door, and looked around bemusedly. "Ah, Sister Wallace!" said Peggy, "A lot has been going on this morning – we'll tell you all about it later. I'm afraid I'm running a bit late with Miss Cavanagh's elevenses!"

Henrietta asked Marie-Colette, "Would you like Sister to check you over, or are you feeling a hundred per cent, now?"

"No need, thank you very much!" was her reply.

The front-door bell rang and Peggy let in Jimmy himself and four policemen, who quickly took charge of the kidnappers.

Chapter 35

Once the policemen had handcuffed their prisoners securely and led them away, Jimmy Manley pointed out that he had brought only plain-clothes officers to make the arrest, and said, "You asked for a Black Maria, but I thought it better to bring a plain van – with any luck we have avoided creating too much of a commotion amongst embassy staff – but we shall see later whether there is any reaction. Please tell me the whole story, someone – I have just come in at the end to find a *fait accompli*! By the way, please give me the guns you took off those two – we might be able to match them with some of the ballistics records we have accumulated at the Yard. Which came from which?"

Alex and Melpomene – who had now put aside her alter ego as Henrietta, feeling more like a detective than a policewoman – or a maid – shared in relating the succession of events, with Peggy adding details here and there – as she said, it felt as though she had been plunged into the best sort of detective story.

When the story was complete, Jimmy said, "I suppose, Walter, that it is not yet particularly late this morning, so it would be good if you could behave normally and just go to your office and get on with your usual work. Perhaps you can keep an eye out for any reactions, particularly in those we are suspicious of – we still have much work to do! But, having said all that, I must congratulate you, Melpomene and Alex, and those two resourceful maids, Muriel and Peggy, for carrying off a very valuable piece of policing! "

"And Marie-Colette, too!" added Melpomene, "She refused to be a victim, even after being grabbed and drugged! Walter is a very lucky man!"

"I know!" said Walter, "I was terrified that I would lose her! I am eternally grateful to all of you! Now, as Jimmy suggests, I am off to work!"

Mel and Alex left the others enthusiastically reliving the adventure, and offered to take Jimmy back to his station. Mel had got so accustomed to her maid's uniform that she quite forgot to change out of it, so when they walked into the flat, Caroline had quite a surprise, but then she remembered to say, "You've had a call a hour ago from Sir Howard Anderson, at the Foreign Office, Mel, I've noted his number – he has something to tell you about Colonel Sharpe, he says."

"That sounds interesting – I'll have a bath and change back into my normal clothes before I telephone him, though."

When Mel rang, Sir Howard said, "I'm afraid I'm going to have to ask you to come to my office, Melpomene – what I have to tell you is rather confidential, and so I can't trust it to an ordinary telephone line. I'll send a car and driver for you, though, so that you will have no trouble getting into the building. When would be convenient?"

"Right now, Howard! I'm quite ready – Alex and I have just had quite an adventure, that I'll tell you about when I see you. Your driver knows where to come? Look forward to talking with you – it all sounds rather intriguing!"

It was no more than fifteen minutes later that the doorbell rang and Caroline opened it to a uniformed chauffeur, who led Melpomene to a black limousine parked outside. Twenty minutes later, she was being ushered into an anonymous building in Whitehall and taken by lift to an upper floor where she was shown into Sir Howard's suite. A woman stood and greeted her, saying, "The Honourable Melpomene Musgrave, I presume?" and took her into Sir Howard's office.

"Come and sit down!" he said, taking her hand, "Would you like a cup of tea?" "Never been known to refuse!" she said, "What is this about – it sounds rather mysterious."

"Yes, I'm afraid we get rather obsessive about secrecy at the FO – please excuse us. I received yesterday a long coded cable sent from Las Palmas in the Canary Isles, where a banana boat, the Santa Katalina, had just docked. As you will readily guess, the message was from Colonel Lionel Sharpe, who you were enquiring about earlier. When I had it decoded, I found that it contained a warning about Brigadier Douglas, the Military Attaché at the St Luke Embassy. Sharpe wanted us to know that Douglas was involved in some serious criminal activity and that he had reason to believe that he was on the verge of precipitating a diplomatic incident that would have dangerous repercussions, not only to St Luke, but to other Caribbean nations and colonies. Sharpe intended to put all the information in his possession at our disposal, but feared that he might not arrive back home in time to avert the happening. His ship is due to dock in Liverpool in three or four days, afterwards sailing to London."

"So, Howard," asked Mel, "am I to assume that you would like us to take some sort of action?"

"Well, yes!" replied Howard, "I know that you are already conducting some sort of investigation at the St Luke Embassy, and I thought you should be forewarned about Douglas. I can't give you the decode of the cable, because we always have to assume that the opposition has intercepted the original. If they got their hands on a decode too, it would be like handing them our code-books wrapped in Christmas paper, with a ribbon round them! So, I'll read it to you and you can make notes – but please make up your own pseudonyms – even names could give them a handle on the code!"

Howard proceeded to do this, and Melpomene promised herself to learn shorthand, as she was close to getting writer's cramp.

Howard had a further piece of information, "I also wanted to tell you that Colonel Sharpe now appears to be firmly on the side of the angels – our investigations have found that his erratic behaviour that caused concern in the British Embassy in St Luke was all to do with activities sanctioned by us at the FO, here in London! This is a classic case of the right hand not being informed of what the left hand is doing!"

"A propos of that, Howard, I should let you know how Walter Huskisson's wife, Marie-Colette, has just been saved from kidnappers! We foiled this attempt and captured the perpetrators, but we have not yet found out who organised this, nor what was the purpose. They demanded a £10,000 ransom, but it is by no means clear that this was the main reason for the abduction."

Melpomene went on to relate the whole story, which entranced Sir Howard. When she had finished, he commented, "I'm inclined to agree with you that the ransom was somewhat of a blind – and with what Sharpe has told me, it's entirely possible that Cedric Douglas is the initiator of the plot. Have you and Alex and Detective-Inspector Manley decided what to do next? If we at the FO can provide any assistance, you have but to mention it!"

"Thank you, Howard, you are very kind, I'll do that!"

Chapter 36

Melpomene asked the chauffeur to take her straight to the office, where she found Alex enthusiastically relating the whole story to an appreciative Marjorie and Winnie.

Alex said, "Jimmy would like you to ring him, Mel – I gather he wants you to assume the guise of WPC Henrietta once more! I hope you never get mixed up between your various roles!"

"I only have the two now, my darling, the housemaid has been retired, so I should be able to keep track – all I will need to do is glance down at my outfit. Please get Jimmy for me, Winnie!"

Jimmy got straight to the point, "If you've recovered enough, I think you should pick up on the two tasks that I assigned to WPC Musgrave. It may be that news of the recent events has already started to circulate around the embassy people, so we should act swiftly before the water becomes muddied! We originally planned for you to call on the Douglas house in the morning, but early afternoon will do as well – but don't delay too much, once you have got into uniform. Get Alex to take you to the area, but park out of sight and watch that nobody spots you getting out of the car – do you remember what we agreed you should do there? "

"Yes, Jimmy, and I kept notes, too!"

"You might notice one or two scruffy characters walking their dog or pushing a pram in the Yeominster Square gardens, but of course, don't acknowledge them! Depending on what happens with Mrs Douglas, you may still be able to fit in a call on Elizabeth O'Connor in the evening – if you do get a chance, please do that. It's getting quite urgent that we find out as much as possible before all the villains are alerted and go into their defensive postures. I needn't remind you to take your pistol!"

"I'm beginning to feel undressed without it, Jimmy! I must also remember to drop my cut-glass accent, if I really have one! Wish me luck – I'll report back when I can."

As planned, WPC Musgrave rang the bell at the Douglas house just after 2 o'clock. Instead of the expected maid, the door was opened by a man in a crumpled suit, with, as Henrietta noticed, a suspicious bulge near his left armpit.

The man said, in a contemptuous drawl, "Collecting for the Police Benevolent Society I s'pose? Or finished showing school-kids acrorst the road for the day, 'ave you?"

"Your mouth's going to get you into trouble sooner or later, chummy!" said Henrietta, "What's more, I hope you've got a licence for whatever it is that's spoiling the drape of your jacket! But I haven't got time now for small talk with small fry. I came here to see Brigadier Douglas about an official complaint that's been received. If he is not here, please let Mrs Douglas know that Constable Musgrave would like to see her – and you can let me in while you're about it, it's chilly on this step!"

The man grimaced but complied, leaving the door open for her to step inside, and disappearing up the staircase. As he left, Henrietta saw something on the back of his head, that could have been a scar. He came back in a minute or two, somewhat abashed, and reluctantly showed her in to a sitting-room. She took a seat and waited for ten minutes, and was just about to go and find someone else, when the door opened and Leonie Douglas entered, looking rather worried.

"How can I help you – is it important? The Brigadier is not at home now," she said, "but we are always ready to do what we can for the police force!"

Henrietta took out her notebook and turned a few pages, then said, in the voice that policemen are reputed to use in court proceedings, "During the course of business yesterday, there was an official complaint lodged at our station by a woman who gave her name as Daisy Sutcliffe, claiming to be a domestic in the service of one of the officers of the St Luke embassy. Are you familiar with this person, Madam?"

"No, I have no dealings with the domestic staff of any of the other houses here, other than being shown in when I visit and being served with afternoon tea and so on. What was the complaint – not about me, I trust?"

"No, Madam, it referred to a Brigadier Cedric Douglas – your husband, I presume. Miss Sutcliffe has made an allegation against him – I will not mention any details as those will be revealed when the complainant and the alleged perpetrator are interviewed formally. So far, no charges have been laid – at the moment, this is merely a complaint. If your husband is not here, I will simply ask you to inform him of this accusation. My Inspector has attempted to reach him at the embassy by telephone, but with no success. He was told that the Brigadier has business that frequently takes him away – a message was taken of course, but there has been no response as yet. That is all I was required to say, Mrs Douglas, so I will take my leave. By the way, who was the person who admitted me this afternoon? He was rather rude to me – maybe you should deter him from such behaviour."

"His name is Hinchcliffe, I believe, but I have nothing to do with him – he works only for my husband – I will mention all this to Cedric when he comes home, which might be quite late – it often is. I'm sure this is all a dreadful mistake, or else an attempt at extortion!"

Melpomene checked round carefully before she approached the Riley and joined Alex.

"That, I hope, has put the cat among the pigeons!" she said, "But as well, I was interested to find that Douglas appears to employ thugs as domestic servants! We should ask Jimmy if he's come across someone called Hinchcliffe – he was carrying something in a shoulder holster, if I'm any judge, and when he turned to go inside, I saw he had a scar on the back of his head."

Back at the office, Mel telephoned Jimmy to report progress. When she had related what had happened, she mentioned Hinchcliffe and his scar.

"You know, Henrietta, we shall have to think about ways of getting finger-prints from people you meet. Those who smoke have an advantage, you can just pass a suspect your cigarette case and put it carefully away afterwards. But your crims these days are getting more and more sophisticated – I blame the boys' magazines for this – Sexton Blake and his like are very popular with the criminal classes, and he has ruined many of the techniques we used to rely on! Burglars know nowadays not to leave clear footprints in garden beds – they wear gloves when they open safes – and they don't sample apples or pieces of cheese when they are peckish and leave them around for the forensic dentists to examine!"

Melpomene added, "But bloodstains are still reliable, aren't they?"

"Surely, Mel" was Jimmy's reply, "but we don't want people to be stabbed just to make the CID's job easier!"

Chapter 37

Jimmy Manley went on, "I'll certainly get Cec Thomson to go through the records, though I doubt whether Hinchcliffe is the guy's real name. The scar on the back of his head might be useful – we shall see! Now, what about WPC Musgrave's other task – do you still intend to visit Elizabeth O'Connor this evening?"

"Oh yes!" said Melpomene, "I thought I'd ask Alex to drive round there after dinner – Mrs M has promised us 'Boof Burbingum', followed by Spotted Dog, so I don't want to miss that! I'll report on progress after my visit – if there's anything worthwhile, that is – should I telephone you at home tonight or leave it until the morning?"

"Leave it until tomorrow, please, Mel. Edith and I are going to the pictures tonight, to see 'His Last Bow' – Sherlock Holmes' last bow, that is. She thinks it might be overdoing things to see detective films after a day's detecting, but I convinced her that Sherlock's methods were more like those of Crabbe and Crabbe than what we humble coppers can muster – it should be a nice relaxing evening!"

As promised, WPC Musgrave was ringing the bell of the O'Connor house at about half-past eight. The door was answered by a maid who was apparently waiting to go to bed, and so was a little snappy with Henrietta, "Madam has already had her bath, so she won't be best pleased at having to talk to the police, but I suppose I will have to go and see whether she has actually gone to bed yet. Please step inside and take a seat – it's too cold to leave the door open."

The maid disappeared up the staircase, and Henrietta could hear her footsteps on the floor above. Then they stopped, and after a few minutes there was a distressed scream! The maid came down a few stairs and called out "Help, please, Miss O'Connor is ill!"

Henrietta ran to join her and was led along the upper hallway to an open bedroom door. Just inside, Elizabeth O'Connor was lying on the floor, face down, with her head on one side, with a dribble of milky fluid coming from her mouth. Henrietta knelt by her and felt her cheek, which was cold – there was no pulse, and she wasn't breathing either – so Henrietta, remembering her St Johns' training at the London School of Economics, tried Holger-Nielson artificial respiration, alternately lifting Elizabeth's arms and pressing on her back, but to no effect.

"You had better call the ambulance," she told the maid, who was weeping freely, "I think it's too late – but call it anyway!"

Henrietta thought she had better have a look around for possible clues. The only thing of note was a tumbler that had rolled under the bed, with a few drops of some milky drink. She carefully wrapped it in a clean handkerchief before picking it up, and put it in her deep jacket pocket.

Henrietta thought that the maid and she both needed a cup of tea, so she asked the maid to take her to the kitchen, "Strong and sweet, please!" she said. While the preparations were being made, she noticed a milk saucepan on the draining board. It had been washed, unfortunately and would not provide any evidence.

"Did Miss O'Connor always have warm milk before retiring?" she asked.

"Yes, with Horlicks – it might have been a bit weak this evening, because there was not much left in the jar. I threw it in the bin."

"I'll take that, please," said Henrietta, "it could be important evidence – you know that in cases like this there has to be a police investigation. Have you had any visitors today?"

"Yes, Miss – Brigadier Douglas and his wife came to dinner, but Mrs Douglas seemed a bit upset. The other maid, Clara White – she only comes in when she's needed – was doing most of the serving, and she told me that it looked as though the Douglas's were having a row! Anyway, they went quite early, nearly an hour before you came."

"Did Clara go home then, too? Can you give me her address, as she might be needed for questions. And what is your name, my dear – you might be wanted for that, too, are you going to stay on here?"

"I'm Margaret Walsh, Miss – I shall have to stay on for as long as I'm needed, and then look for another position – I come from the Midlands, and all my family are there – but I want to stay in London, it suits me better! I'll write Clara's address down for you – and her telephone number – she had it put on so she could be called up for waitressing – she does it for others in the Embassy, too."

It was over half an hour before the ambulance men arrived. They inspected the patient, but again could find no pulse, so they lifted her onto the bed.

"We'll have to take her to Finchley hospital," the senior of the two men said, "for an examination to determine the cause of death. Please tell us your names, they'll want to know who to contact."

Henrietta and the maid did so, and asked that Detective-Inspector Manley, at Mile End Road station, be informed too.

At these reminders of her mistress' death, the maid broke into sobs again. Henrietta asked where the telephone was, rang the North Finchley police, and said she'd wait at the house till they came, which only took them ten minutes. Then she explained what had happened and handed over to them and walked back to the car, finding Alex asleep at the wheel. He started when she woke him up, so she said, "It's a good job it was me and not some villain! You've missed some high drama, you know! I'll tell you all about it!"

After she had related the story, she went on, "I expect the real police will want to examine the scene," she said, "but we'll probably have to wait for a post-mortem – there were no signs of violence that I could see, and I could detect no obvious signs of poisoning, chloroform or anything. I know what chloroform smells like, as you can well recall! She had drunk some Horlicks, so I kept the jar and the tumbler she had used, for analysis and for fingerprints, though the maid and Elizabeth O'Connor would have both handled them pretty comprehensively."

"Of course," said Alex, "she could have died of natural causes – we shouldn't assume that every sudden death is murder, just because we're in the trade!"

"Or it could have been suicide," said Mel, "a quick glass of something, and into bed – it might have acted more quickly than she expected. She was dressed in a nightie, with a peignoir over it, so it looks as though she was on her way to bed."

"No doubt this will all be resolved when we hear the results of the autopsy," said Alex, "let's sleep on it and stop worrying until then."

Chapter 38

Melpomene and Alex took their time over breakfast, scanning the morning paper eagerly – but there was no story about Elizabeth O'Connor yet. Alex telephoned Jimmy too, but he had not heard from the hospital either. Mel asked whether she should send him the tumbler and Horlicks jar for forensic examination, but he said there was no hurry – and anyway their importance as evidence depended on the cause of death.

They both felt a little let down by the absence of action and decided to drive to the office. "Don't forget to cover your hair, Mel!" Alex reminded her.

When they arrived at Crabbe and Crabbe, they related the events of the day to a rapt Winnie and Marjorie over the statutory tea and jam tarts.

"What with the rescue of Madame Huskisson, and the demise of Miss O'Connor," said Marjorie, "life at this agency is becoming almost too exciting! I think we shall feel rather let down if the routine returns to normal! By the way, we did have an enquiry yesterday which sounded as though it was in Alex' area. I wrote it up – shall I give you my notes, Alex?"

He took the folder and read it through, nodding from time to time. "This seems as though it could become interesting, Mel," he said, "the proprietor of a hotel not a hundred miles from here suspects that his chief of staff has been running a lucrative call-girl service out of his establishment! Perhaps I will offer to pose as a prospective customer – a prosperous businessman feeling rather lonely on a working trip to London, or something of the sort!"

"You certainly will not!" said Melpomene, "There are other ways to approach this – and I'm not prepared to play the part of one of his ladies, either! Does the enquirer want it stopped, or does he simply want a slice of the profits?"

"Why don't we just decline to take the job?" said Alex, "Since the entire resources of the police force, backed up with legislation, have never been able to stop this sort of thing, we would be foolish to even try!"

"Hear, hear!" said Melpomene, "Please call him, Marjorie, and politely refuse to take the case! No need to give a reason!"

"As well as awaiting the post-mortem results on Elizabeth O'Connor," said Alex, "it would be interesting to know whether Jimmy and his boys have turned up anything about Macnamara and Rowley, either through cross-examination or from criminal records – and there's Hinchcliffe as well! I imagine they will let us know promptly – they have always done so in the past."

"That reminds me," said Melpomene, "I should let Howard Anderson, at the Foreign Office, know about my visit to the Douglas house, even though the Brigadier was not there. I'll mention Hinchcliffe, too – it's possible that Howard might have heard of him. And, of course, the unexpected demise of Elizabeth O'Connor might very likely interest him as well, especially as we were told that the Brigadier and his wife had dined with her earlier that evening! Was it Walter Scott who said, *'Oh what a tangled web we weave, When first we practice to deceive.'*?"

Alex asked, "So was there anything about either Douglas or O'Connor in that coded cable from Lionel Sharpe? I haven't had much of a chance to peruse your scribbled notes, yet, Mel – you really must go on a short-hand course, soon!"

"As far as I can recall, Alex, O'Connor didn't feature, but Sharpe certainly had plenty of dirt on Douglas! Currency deals were mentioned, especially large amounts in Swiss and Italian banknotes as well as Sterling, of course, travelling in both directions, but mainly towards the Americas. Howard Anderson was going to make further enquiries, of course. Given his obsession with security, he might want me to visit his office to discuss all this privately, so I'd better give him a call."

"Meanwhile, "said Alex, "I'll try Jimmy to see what news he has of the two foolish desperados who tried to kidnap Marie-Colette! It would have been interesting to see how she would have fared had we not intervened. Bashed the first one senseless with the chamber-pot, grabbed his gun and dispatched the second with it and then calmly rung the police, would be my guess!"

When Melpomene spoke to Howard Anderson the only update he had for her was that he had heard that the *Santa Katalina* had been diverted directly to Tilbury, without calling at Liverpool, due to arrive on next morning's tide. So Mel said she would let both Detective-Inspector Manley and Senior Preventive Officer

Fisher of Customs know, so that they could arrange to whisk Lionel Sharpe away safely, in case the crooks had got wind of his arrival. "Very wise, Melpomene!" said Howard, "It is quite likely that they have been set all of a flurry by Madame Huskisson's rescue and might resort to something desperate to have him silenced!"

"And I have some related items of interest for you, too!" said Mel, and proceeded to describe her, perhaps fruitless, visit to the Douglas residence, followed by the far more interesting account of her discovery of the demise of Elizabeth O'Connor later that day.

"As I was just remarking," said Howard Anderson, "I would not be at all surprised if Cedric Douglas panicked when visited by a policewoman and decided, there and then, that Miss O'Connor would be better out of the way. Am I right in recalling that she had entertained the Douglas couple to dinner after you had been making enquiries of Mrs Douglas, ostensibly prompted by a complaint about the Brigadier?"

"You are right, and of course," explained Melpomene, "both of my visits in the garb of a policewomen were intended by Jimmy Manley not only to find out what I could, but also to sow seeds of suspicion in the minds of those we have suspected of being involved in the conspiracy that is running in diplomatic circles!"

"So," said Howard, "that makes it more urgent for us to take whatever measures we can to forestall any further activities they may be planning. I will make arrangements to have extra precautions taken to safeguard Colonel Sharpe when the *Santa Katalina* docks tomorrow. Maybe I can get one of my armed officers put aboard when the ship picks up the pilot, at Gravesend or wherever it will be tomorrow. I will get onto Trinity House immediately and find out when and where the pilot will be taken on board. Leave that to me, Melpomene! We'll try to have Sharpe tucked up somewhere safe so you can talk to him, as I guess you're dying to do!"

"Very good, Howard! And if his daughter Janice could meet him there, they would both be very grateful! I'm sure that this would set Janice's mind at ease like nothing else! She was the one who prompted all our investigations into diplomatic circles in the first place, and we have had to keep her in the dark ever since, poor child!"

Chapter 39

When Melpomene rang off she turned to tell Alex all about it, only to find him still talking animatedly – to Jimmy, she supposed – but as she listened, she realized it was not the Detective-Inspector but someone else.

When he hung up, she asked "Who was that, Alex – I thought you were going to ask Jimmy about further developments?"

"I was about to telephone him when Adrian Fitz-Hugh called us to give us some very interesting news! He and Hugo Palance have been investigating a gun-running cartel operating between metropolitan France and corrupt officials in the French Embassies in Jamaica and Cuba. He told me that they – the authorities, that is – have been allowing them to run uninterrupted while they built up ways of keeping them under surveillance. And – surprise, surprise! – a certain Brigadier Douglas shows up as a key figure in the English branch of the cartel. Our Foreign Office friend, Howard Anderson, has been liaising with Adrian over this, and has passed him much of the information that was in the coded cable from Lionel Sharpe. And, Mel, Adrian would like us both to go and meet with him and Hugo and a couple of others, as they have been brewing up plans for action that include us!"

"When will this be?" asked Melpomene, "Should we do anything in preparation?"

"I think not, Mel, since he is sending a car to pick us up in half an hour!"

"So there is just enough time to have more tea and jam tarts! Could you oblige, please, Winnie?"

Within an hour, Mel and Alex were being shown into the special department at Scotland Yard, where they were greeted warmly but formally by Adrian Fitz-Hugh, and more enthusiastically by Hugo Palance, who folded Mel in a bear-hug, kissing her on both cheeks. They were then introduced to another member of the group, a tall saturnine figure with a pronounced limp, called Commodore David Evans.

"Call me Taffy!" he said in a pronounced Welsh accent, "Everybody else does! I'm supposed to be invalided out of the Royal Navy, but they have found me hard to get rid of, so I've been seconded to this group as Naval liaison. I let people assume I hurt me leg in a battle at sea, but really it was just a sea-water ulcer that got out of hand! If your mam tells you to keep your socks dry, you should take heed of her!"

After a little more chit-chat over coffee and cakes, Adrian called the group to order. "Alex Crabbe has told me a little of his and your recent exploits, Melpomene, but I invite you to give this group the benefit of your account, starting with the attempted kidnap of Marie-Colette Huskisson."

Melpomene went straight ahead, with occasional additions and amendments from Alex, until she finished by describing the sad case of Elizabeth O'Connor, "We still haven't heard whether the cause of death has been established – maybe it would not be too early to try telephoning Jimmy Manley again?"

"Good idea, Mel!" said Adrian, and beckoning to one of the two secretaries who had been keeping shorthand notes of the meeting, asked, "Annette, my dear, could you try to get Detective-Inspector Manley for us?"

With little delay, she passed the telephone to him, saying, "DI Manley for you, Deputy Commissioner."

There were a few moments of social catch-up remarks and then a more serious conversation after which Adrian said, "Excellent, Jimmy, I have that. I'll just pass it to the others and see whether they want to ask you anything else, hang on, please."

"The results of the autopsy are in now, and show clearly that Miss O'Connor died from a dose of sodium cyanide, probably administered in her warm Horlicks drink. Jimmy says that Melpomene has kept both the tumbler the lady used and the nearly-empty Horlicks jar, so it will be straightforward to determine whether indeed that was the way she was poisoned. Finding the culprit is quite another matter, but we know that Douglas was in the house earlier that evening, so making a connection is tempting! More investigation follows!"

There was an immediate buzz of conversation around the table at this news, Alex saying, "I hope you put the evidence away safely, Mel – it would be a disaster if the glass and bottle were to be washed up in a fit of enthusiastic cleaning!"

"No fear of that. I locked them both in the drawer of my bureau in the flat! I have the key with me right now." said Mel, "I'll get them taken to the appropriate lab as soon as possible."

Adrian took the telephone again, saying, "Still there Jimmy? Mel will get that evidence to wherever you want it, as soon as she can. Now, would you like to tell us what, if anything, you have turned up about the various villains, Hinchcliffe, Macnamara and Rowley? Really – all three of them? What a demonstration of loyalty! Were there any more? Have you discovered any sort of headquarters they may have been using? I'll tell the others, and it would be good if you could bring all your notes here and we can consolidate all our information – would it suit you to come here straight away? Good, Jimmy, look forward to seeing you soon."

He rang off and announced, "All three of those individuals were at one time or another in Brigadier Douglas' unit within the Rutland Light Infantry, along with the notorious Reg Withers, the man who was so misguided as to try to kidnap Melpomene! Jimmy has asked the War Office to supply him with regimental records for the last few years – there well might have been more of their comrades enlisted by Douglas for his own private army!"

Hugo Palance was grinning widely, saying, "*C'est formidable, ça!* These idiots are all following the same pattern! One of the leaders of the French arm of the organization we have recently identified as Brevet-Colonel Henri Mercier, who commanded a company of sappers during the recent war and has brought half-a-dozen of them into the game. Sappers, you may realize, are often highly skilled in signals and in infiltration, naturally becoming expert safe-crackers! Most of them also developed during the war a taste for daring exploits and find peace-time rather boring!"

Then Adrian said, "Since Jimmy Manley is coming, we can leave the discussion of these foot-soldiers until he is here, but I'd like to bring everyone up to the present with what we have found out about Brigadier Cedric Douglas – especially as he is emerging as a candidate for the role of chief murderer. Melpomene and Alex know that Lionel Sharpe has already provided us with some useful evidence by cable, and we are all looking forward to speaking with him when he docks tomorrow. So, all in all, we remain in no doubt that Douglas is the principal active participant, if not the chief of operations."

Chapter 40

While they were waiting for Detective-Inspector Manley to arrive, the discussion continued. Alex asked, "We have now heard about two leading lights of the cabal – Cedric Douglas and Henri Mercier – perhaps you could tell us, Adrian, whether there are any others in similar positions? And this begs the question as to whether there are those above them in the hierarchy. But, you were about to tell us more about Douglas, Adrian – I'm sorry if I've broken your chain of thought!"

"Not at all, Alex! Apart from what Colonel Sharpe listed in his cable, we have other sources of information. Like Sharpe, all military attachés cannot resist being professionally suspicious of their counterparts in rival embassies, in the same city and elsewhere. It is my notion that they all yearn to be active players in the "Great Game" although this may simply reflect delusions of grandeur! Anyway, whatever the underlying psychology, we at the FO have received documents, mostly unattributed and from anonymous sources, which seem to detail instances of dishonest behaviour by Brigadier Douglas."

He picked up a folder, thumbed through it and took out an envelope, saying, "Here is a typical example, received through the ordinary mails, some four weeks ago. It is hand-addressed simply to 'Foreign Office, London', it bears the correct stamp, and is post-marked W8, which is not far from Yeominster Square. What it contains is a bunch of pages from a common memo pad, listing items such as bundles of banknotes, consigned by someone with the initials 'CD', carrying code numbers and letters – looking to me like the serial numbers of diplomatic bags – and with pencilled remarks, such as, 'v. imp'. There are a number of similar envelopes here."

Melpomene spoke up, "Please show these to Jimmy when he comes – I fancy that they might be the very same envelopes that one of his watchers saw handed over every day by a maid from the chief chancery clerk's household to a courier waiting for them in the Yeominster Square gardens. We have been dying to find out what they were all about ever since!"

Adrian exclaimed, "Oh my goodness! It is only this moment that I recall you asking me about possibilities for intercepting that mail – I failed to make the connection until now! And all the time these envelopes were being sent here without the need for us to lift a finger! I wonder who it was who decided that Douglas needed this attention – the fact that it was one of the chancery clerk's maids who made the deliveries is not terribly significant. As we've found out recently, there is a lot of traffic across back gardens amongst the domestic sisterhood!"

Melpomene had been getting fidgety during these statements, and then asked, in a frustrated tone of voice, "It appears to me that we have now accumulated firm evidence that Brigadier Douglas has been up to no good for years! And we also have reasonable suspicion that he is behind the recent series of criminal acts – my own foiled kidnap, the aborted attempt on Marie-Colette and, most recently, the presumed murder of Elizabeth O'Connor! When are we going to pin him down for these, and how? Surely we can't just let him carry on unchecked, especially as he seems to be picking on women the whole time?"

Said Alex, "Let's wait until Jimmy gets here, Mel! It's quite likely he is working on a number of practical approaches while we've been speculating. Perhaps the famous Horlicks jar and tumbler will have Douglas' prints on them – though he is probably too fly a bird to be caught that way! And let me pick up on a query I had earlier – what have you got on this Mercier character, Hugo?"

Hugo Palance was eager to answer.

"In fact, Alex *mon ami*, we have the Brevet Colonel on an even tighter rein than Brigadier Douglas – however, as Adrian will tell you, I think that even le brave Cedric can be gathered up at a moment's notice. We know Henri Mercier's headquarters and place of residence, in Calais; we are maintaining constant surveillance on it, to the extent that we can stretch out the long arm of the Sûreté and grasp him or any of his confrères whenever we so desire. The longer we keep them under observation, the more we learn about their operations – and even more important – about their confederates. We have operatives poised ready to strike at a word, and in fact the zero hour is not far off! You, Melpomene and Alex, will be among the first to know when we finally strike!"

Melpomene was about to question Hugo further, when there was a tap on the door, and a young woman approached Adrian and murmured in his ear. "By all means!" he told her, and she ushered in none other than Jimmy Manley, accompanied by a drably-dressed man who was recognized immediately by Mel.

"Mr Hinchcliffe!" she exclaimed with a gasp, and reached into her handbag.

Jimmy Manley raised both hands, saying, "No need to take violent action Mel – may I introduce Detective-Sergeant Alastair Robson, who has been working undercover for the Met for the past three years! As another ex-member of the Rutland Light Infantry, he managed to talk himself into a job on Douglas' staff. As you might well imagine, he is now a treasury of information about the Brigadier and his activities, to the point that he was able to set him up to be arrested this very afternoon!"

Consternation all round! Everyone started talking at once, including Melpomene, whose somewhat piercing voice was able to penetrate the general hubbub, saying, "Congratulations to Alastair! Will you still need the Horlicks jar and the tumbler, Jimmy?"

"Oh, yes, Mel! I've rarely seen a more resourceful interviewee under interrogation than Cedric Douglas, so he will be very hard to pin down – but we now have, as well as all the documentary and circumstantial evidence, a small bottle of Sodium Cyanide crystals found several weeks ago in Douglas' desk drawer by Alastair Robson, during one of his systematic searches, and doctored by him with a light admixture of Boric Acid, which is easily identified under analysis. Regrettably this poison was administered before Alastair realized it was to be used in earnest on Elizabeth O'Connor! But it should be straightforward to detect traces of both chemicals in the jar and tumbler."

"What were the results of the autopsy?", asked Alex, "Were the same substances found in the stomach contents?"

"Certainly! Although the pathologist didn't spot the boric acid until it was suggested it be looked for – but now we have a chain of evidence linking them both with Douglas! I doubt whether we shall find fingerprints, so we shall need that connection. I have no doubt that our doughty Brigadier will engage one of London's best criminal King's Counsels and a complete team for his defence, so we will need all the advantages that we can muster!"

Chapter 41

The meeting was brought to a conclusion by an attendant announcing that supper was served in an adjacent room, courtesy of Adrian Fitz-Hugh, giving Hugo Palance and Taffy Evans a chance to talk informally with Mel and Alex and swap their recent experiences.

Hugo had heard a little about the kidnap attempts on both Melpomene and Marie-Colette, but wanted all the details. He was especially tickled to hear how each of them had cast aside any tendencies to lady-like behaviour, "What is it that your Rudyard Kipling says so effectively about the female of the species? My favourite stanza runs like this: *'When the Himalayan peasant meets the he-bear in his pride,/He shouts to scare the monster who will often turn aside./But the she-bear thus accosted rends the peasant tooth and nail,/For the female of the species is more deadly than the male.'* "

"I'm not sure that Marie-Colette and I would entirely like that particular analogy!" said Melpomene, "But I will accept the reference gracefully!"

Taffy was highly amused, but declined to contribute a literary allusion of his own, saying, "I'm afraid that our naval ditties are not at all suitable for mixed company, no matter how robust the ladies might be!"

Alex brought the conversation back to more practical matters, "What arrangements have been made to meet Lionel Sharpe?" he asked, "Should either or both of us come to Tilbury?"

"Ah, I haven't yet brought you up to date about that," replied Jimmy, "what with all the excitement about nabbing Douglas. Over the last few hours, coded cables have been flashing back and forth, and the current plan is that Colonel Sharpe will be taken off the *Santa Katalina* by the pilot boat at Gravesend. Even though we now know that Cedric Douglas has been rendered *hors de combat*, it still seemed necessary to take every precaution to keep Sharpe safe – after all, he is going to be a vital witness in several other matters. Stephen and Eugenie Buckmaster have kindly offered to put him up at their home in Woodhampton – but we're not advertising this – and Janice will join him there soon, since it is nearly the end of term at Hillyard House."

Adrian Fitz-Hugh nodded, but had something more to say, "First of all, though, once he has been successfully plucked from the banana boat, he will be taken to a Foreign Office establishment in the countryside near Canterbury, where Howard Anderson and I and some experts from Scotland Yard and the Foreign Office will debrief him at length. Howard and I would really like you both, Melpomene and Alex, to join us there. The place is an old stately home, which is often used as a retreat or conference centre. When we are not being busy, you will find pleasant things to do there."

After a while, as it was getting quite late, Jimmy offered to take Melpomene and Alex back to their flat, "I'll pick up that evidence, too! I'm really looking forward to seeing Douglas in the dock, accompanied by several of his minions who will be charged with deprivation of liberty, assault with a deadly weapon and other assorted crimes, but I assume preparation of all of those cases will take some weeks yet."

Back at the flat, Melpomene invited Jimmy and Alastair Robson to come in and join them over a cup of tea.

"In my mind," she said, "I'm still puzzled about those envelopes. Someone in the know must have gone to considerable trouble to put that evidence together, but who? We know that they were given to the courier by a maid from the household of the chancery clerk, but this doesn't really signify, as all the maids seem to fraternize freely. How should we go about finding out?"

"Let's talk to Walter Huskisson first," said Alex, "we need to bring him up to date about everything anyway, now that Douglas is behind bars. I'll telephone him at home in the morning."

Alastair Robson said, "Maybe I can help you here, too. Playing the role of a domestic servant gave me no official access to the chancery building, of course, but procedures are not always adhered to, even in the best-managed establishments. All validated personnel are supposed to wear an official badge at all times, but those with senior status often dispense with this, since they are known to and recognized by almost everyone, and send their servants on errands, whenever they feel like it. For example, only two days ago, Douglas telephoned his wife and asked her – rather, I should say, instructed her – to tell me to bring him a file folder he had forgotten to take with him in the morning. This sort of thing was not at all unusual."

"But," asked Melpomene, "Walter told us that all documents moving into and out of each office in the embassy are carefully recorded, are they not?"

"In theory, yes, of course," said Alastair, "and there are clerks stationed near all the entrances whose duty is to keep such records – but often they simply wave people and items through, especially when they are busy on other duties. But, I have switched to generalities when I really meant to give you some specific information about those envelopes. I'm pretty sure that it was Desmond McPhail who was responsible – but you should ask him, rather that relying on my guesswork – he is a decent person, as Walter Huskisson would tell you. Brigadier Douglas, on the other hand, regards him as a weakling – which is another recommendation in my book!"

"What is the situation now in the Douglas household, now he has been arrested?" asked Melpomene, "is Leonie Douglas staying at the embassy, do you know?"

"I have no idea, I'm afraid, Melpomene, you will have to make enquiries next time you talk to Walter Huskisson or Desmond McPhail. I have no intention of going back there myself! I shall see you again at the Foreign Office retreat, no doubt. It has been very pleasant making your acquaintance!"

At that, he and Jimmy made their farewells, Jimmy saying that arrangements would be made the next day to take Mel and Alex to the retreat. "I should bring one of your delightful secretaries with you," he added, "no doubt you will want comprehensive notes made of the proceedings, and the official transcript might be a while in preparation."

As soon as the guests had left, Mel had a quick bath and flung herself into bed, "Not before eight o'clock, please, Alex – but not long after, either! It looks as though we're up for yet another busy day tomorrow!"

"I'll set the alarm and leave a note for Caroline, too!" said Alex, "I would hate to miss anything, now we have got so far! I don't suppose young Janice will get much sleep tonight – but maybe I'm underestimating the resilience of the young! Goodnight, my love – see you in the morning!"

There was no response!

Chapter 42

Straight after breakfast, Melpomene and Alex drove to the Crabbe and Crabbe office. They told Winnie and Marjorie all about their meeting at Scotland Yard, and explained about the arrangements for meeting Colonel Sharpe at the Foreign Office retreat.

"We've been asked to bring one of you along, to take notes of the proceedings," said Alex, "do you want to toss for it or draw straws or something? It will probably take all day."

Winnie and Marjorie put their heads together, and then Winnie announced, "I'll go, please, if that's all right! Marjorie is a little under the weather today, so she will have to go on another occasion, whenever there is one. When are we going?"

"Jimmy is going to send a car for us, "said Mel, "we're not quite sure when – it depends when Lionel Sharpe gets picked up by the pilot boat – it's not far from Gravesend to Canterbury. We'll just have to wait for a call. Make sure you take plenty of shorthand notebooks and pencils with you, Winnie."

"What if I need to get in touch with you during the day?" asked Marjorie, "do you have a telephone number for the retreat?"

"No, but you can ring Mile End Road station and they will tell you."

It was less than an hour later that DC Cec Thomson arrived at the door and asked if they were ready to go, saying that he had just heard from Jimmy Manley that the operation at Gravesend had gone smoothly and that Colonel Sharpe was rather relieved at his interception, since he had been getting quite anxious about possible retaliation, not only from the Douglas faction, but from other criminal organizations involved. "We'll learn all about this when we see him, no doubt!"

In the car, Cec explained that Jimmy and one of Howard Anderson's assistants had taken charge of meeting the pilot boat and were driving Sharpe straight to Crowminster Hall. "They tell me that it's a palatial manor house in the old style – when it's not being used for retreats like ours it functions something like a country club, with a nine-hole golf course, horse-riding, and tennis courts in the summer, too. Foreign

Office officials above a certain rank can take their families there for holidays."

The driver knew the way to Crowminster Hall and the roads were clear, so they were soon arriving at the Hall. As they drew up at the front steps, Jimmy Manley came out of the front door and anxiously waited for them to get out of the car.

"Urgent news, Mel and Alex!" he said, "We've just had a message from Walter Huskisson – Desmond McPhail has been shot! Come inside and I'll tell you the whole story!"

They were led to a sitting-room, where Howard Anderson and Adrian Fitz-Hugh were talking animatedly with a small group, including a well-set up gentleman with a moustache, who was introduced as Colonel Sharpe.

"Anything further about Desmond?" asked Jimmy, before the others could say any more, to which Fitz-Hugh answered, "McPhail has been operated upon in hospital and it doesn't seem quite as bad as we had feared. He has taken two shots to the chest, but happily they missed his vital organs, though his right lung has suffered what they call a pneumothorax, which means a collapsed lung. They have inserted a tube and say that it is under control. He is under a general anaesthetic, while the bullets are removed and the wounds attended to, so will be in no condition to talk for twelve hours or so!"

"So what happened?" asked Melpomene, "Was it in the embassy, or what?"

"What I was told was this," said Jimmy, "Desmond was on his way to work, taking his normal short walk – out of his front garden and the few yards to the main embassy entrance. Apparently he was shutting his gate when two men got out of a car, shot him and made off – apparently they had a driver waiting with the engine running. We know all this, because two young clerks were on their way to work at the chancery building and saw it all. One tried to see whether she could help him at all, while the other ran in and raised the alarm. An ambulance arrived within ten minutes or so and took charge, rendering what first aid they could and then taking him to the emergency department."

"Did anybody get a good look at these assassins?" asked Mel, "Were any of your surveillance team on the job, Jimmy?"

"Yes, and I'm rather proud of this!" was the answer, "WDC Valerie Morton was taking her dressed-up doll for his morning walk in his perambulator in the gardens right opposite. She missed the main action, but as a well-trained detective got the make and number of the car and a description of both assailants – but not of the driver. We're working on these details back at Mile End Road now."

Adrian Fitz-Hugh spoke up, "As you may imagine, this has confirmed the necessity for Colonel Sharpe to be guarded assiduously! The intent of the shooting was obviously to prevent McPhail from disclosing what he has accumulated concerning the illicit activities of Brigadier Douglas, and Lionel here has even more of that information!"

"So you'd better interview me exhaustively before they bump me off too!" said Sharpe, "I have written a lot of it up already, but it needs someone who knows all the background to make sense of all the individual facts. That's where you investigators, both police and private, can be most valuable, in my opinion."

Alex had further thoughts, "Are there any others, at the embassy or elsewhere, who are in danger? It looks as though these gangsters, or whoever they are, will stop at nothing to cover up their tracks. I imagine that Desmond McPhail is going to be looked after somewhere – I don't want to know where!"

Melpomene agreed, "They have already had a crack at Marie-Colette Huskisson – presumably this was aimed at pressuring Walter – so do we need to put him into quarantine as well? If we are not careful, we'll be nurse-maiding almost all the personnel at the embassy, to say nothing of Alex and me and our staff! And while we're about it, should we take account of our allies in France and elsewhere? We know that Hugo Palance and the Sûreté are following parallel investigations to those of Scotland Yard – isn't that right, Adrian?"

"Melpomene makes an important point!" said Adrian, "We know that the diverse gangs that make up the cabal are all in constant communication, so there is every reason to believe that they will collaborate whenever they have a common aim. And the elimination of hostile witnesses is a matter that must concern them all. I suggest that we all take refreshments – I know I need something – and then convene a plenary session to first work out a draft agenda and then start addressing individual issues."

Chapter 43

After they had tea or coffee and snacks, they were all led into a conference-room and seated around a large table, Adrian Fitz-Hugh taking the chair.

"I have just been telephoning my department," he announced, "and found that Commissaire Principal Palance and Commodore Evans were still reachable, so I have left a message inviting them to join us here. I hope that we might see them here in a couple of hours. There may be others whose contribution would be valuable, like Jens-Olle Pedersen, but it would be premature to try to involve them just yet, I think. If anyone has others in mind who could be of immediate help, please suggest them."

Howard Anderson spoke up, "My thoughts turn to Chief Inspector Saunders, of the Fraud Squad, and Ben Fisher, of the Customs at Tilbury, who have helped in the past, when we were concentrating on art dealings. Would it be worth while involving them at this stage, or should we hold them in reserve, so to speak?"

Fitz-Hugh nodded, "Saunders should be asked now, I think, and Fisher later, maybe. We run the risk of unduly complicating the business if we are not careful. Now, let us see whether we can identify a small number of burning issues that we need to address first. I would suggest that dealing with potential dangers to our witnesses must take pride of place, starting by identifying who they are and who are suspected to be threats to them. Fortunately we have already taken care of Douglas himself, but we must assume he has a number of underlings to call upon, like those we have already seen in action, including the attack on McPhail this morning."

Alex spoke up, "I'm still unclear how it became possible to pick up Douglas and how it was done. Could someone enlighten me, if it can be done quickly and easily?"

"I can do that," said Jimmy Manley, "I'm so full of it myself that I have been assuming I told everyone! Detective-Sergeant Alastair Robson, aka Hinchcliffe, had managed to persuade Douglas that he was a loyal subordinate, to the point that yesterday the brigadier took him aside and ordered him to smother Mrs Douglas – yes, his own wife – with a pillow, as soon as she went to sleep that evening, having taken her usual sleeping draught. Alastair said, 'So are you ordering me to murder Mrs Douglas?' to which Douglas replied angrily, 'Yes, you fool!' Then Alastair seized him in a ju-jitsu hold, handcuffed him to his desk chair and told him he was under arrest for uttering deadly threats. My men were soon on the scene to take him away!"

Said Melpomene, "We suspected this character was a psychopath – at least, I did! – and now we know! I suppose he thought that his wife had enough on him to constitute a danger! And I would like to point out Walter Huskisson as another person in need of protection. They have already tried to kidnap Marie-Colette, and we must assume that this was a way of applying pressure on Walter. The ransom demand, I think we all agreed, was not the main point but a diversion."

"What about the men who shot Desmond this morning?" asked Adrian Fitz-Hugh, "You said your policewoman got the make and number of the car, Jimmy, has there been any progress in tracking it down?"

"We should ask Cec Thomson," said Jimmy, "he's been keeping in touch with Mile End Road since he got here. Any news, Cec?"

"Well, yes, but rather a disappointment, I'm afraid – the car, a Singer saloon, was reported stolen last night from outside a pub in Stepney, and was found abandoned near Marylebone tube station an hour ago, by a PC checking on illegal parking. It has been towed to Mile End Road for fingerprinting and examination, but we've heard nothing further. Of course it's pretty pointless looking for witnesses. We've also had an interim report from the hospital – Desmond has been taken off the critical list, but is still in the intensive care unit, heavily sedated. The sister in charge tells me that he will probably be roused tomorrow morning, unless there are any setbacks. But she says that the surgeon will probably not want him questioned until he is completely happy with his progress."

"In any case," said Jimmy, "he won't be able to tell us much about his assailants unless he actually recognized one or both of them, which seems unlikely! But once they've been caught and charged it will be useful if he can identify them, I suppose."

Adrian Fitz-Hugh reminded the group that they were trying to list those under threat from the gangs. "They would have no reason, I suppose, to go after the Ambassador or his wife, nor yet the head of Chancery nor the Chief of Protocol, but I'm a bit bothered about the other officer with direct responsibility for cash transactions, meaning Desmond's nominal superior, Cyril Sidmouth, the comptroller. The gang might well assume that, since Desmond was documenting Douglas' illicit transactions, Sidmouth might well know something about them, too. So Howard – as a Foreign Office representative – how would you feel about dropping a word of warning to him? And once he is informed, should we detail an armed policeman to watch over his family? He should be safe enough within the Embassy, given that there are security people constantly on duty there."

Howard Anderson was looking more and more uncomfortable, remarking, "This is showing all the signs of developing into a serious diplomatic incident! My only consolation is that St Luke is only a minnow swimming in the diplomatic ocean – but even such a minnow has the power to make waves! Oh dear, my metaphors are getting completely out of hand!"

Melpomene raised her hand and made a suggestion, "Let us try to put these weighty issues aside – we have far more practical matters that we need to deal with, such as finding these gunmen and other heavies – it would be really useful if we had any idea of the location of their various hang-outs or headquarters. Could we, for instance, try to locate the shed I was being taken to when I shot my captor in the hand? It sounded to me at the time as though this was a hide-out, where the so-called 'cleaning services' and other mysterious characters were located. I can remember the laneway we were driving through when I plugged the guy – could we arrange to get a search done for that shed? They wouldn't refer to it as a shed if it were, say, a warehouse or a factory, would they? If someone went for a poke round, they might be able to come up with some possibilities."

"Very good, Mel," said Fitz-Hugh, "and a task of similar scope would be to try to ferret out some more of the gang members. If we have a thorough look at those we've already got locked up, we might be able to get an idea of where to start looking for their associates. We could start with ex-members of Douglas' military unit who now live in the London area. Perhaps Alastair, you might have come across some of them when you were pretending to be one of their company?"

"Of course!" said Alastair, "Some of us used to meet in a pub!"

Chapter 44

"Surely you must be joking, Alastair!" said Alex, "Do you mean ex-comrades from your old regiment, or members of Douglas' gang?"

"Some of each, actually!" said Alastair, "Ostensibly our meetings were in the nature of regimental reunions, where we bragged about our exploits in the war and shared other reminiscences over many rounds of beer and games of darts or shove-ha'penny, but from time to time a small group, sometimes including me, would gather in a corner and receive our orders, from a man we used to refer to as 'the adjutant'. He had been, I think, on the Brigadier's staff in the army – he certainly seemed still to occupy a position of authority. Once I had become a member of the Douglas household I took orders straight from the Brigadier, but on earlier occasions I was given instructions hand-written by the adjutant."

"Yes!" said Melpomene, "We have seen such a note! Maybe you can explain some of the parts of it that were puzzling us. They were the instructions given to the guy who was supposed to kidnap me – I managed to stop him by shooting him in the hand, so he is in hospital under guard now. In that note there were references to people called 'whistler' and 'cabinet maker', and it mentions 'cleaning services' as well as saying that my planned destination was 'the shed'. Finally, it was signed 'Grannie' or 'Graham' – the writing was too bad to tell which! Does any of this mean anything to you, Alastair?"

"Some of it does, certainly!" replied Alastair, "The signature is neither 'Grannie' nor 'Graham', but 'Garrison', short for 'Garrison Adjutant' – most of the time we just called him 'Adjutant'. As for 'whistler', that's an old Army term for 'lookout' – someone who gives a signal when a target is spotted – you in that case, Melpomene!"

"I thought that might be the case!" said Mel, "What about 'cabinet maker' and 'cleaning services'?"

"No idea, sorry! Maybe they would have meant something to your kidnapper. But you are right about the 'shed' – I've actually been there, and I'm pretty sure I can find my way back there if you really want!"

Adrian Fitz-Hugh asked, "Alastair – have you any reason to suppose that your cover has been blown, now? It looks as though you could be very valuable to us if you are still regarded as a gang member by the others."

"I think I shall still be trusted, Deputy Commissioner, there's no way that Douglas could have fingered me to the others – he has been in secure custody since I nabbed him – and nobody else would know what has happened. I've been working undercover on this and previous cases for quite a while, and I know what signs to look out for. I'm certainly prepared to talk to or point out my former companions at the 'Builders Arms', or to take anyone to the shed, whatever you wish!"

"Very good! This will all be very useful – we'll work out a plan of campaign. Tomorrow would be best, the shorter the time that elapses the better. Now let us turn our attention elsewhere! We've already raised the question of keeping Cyril Sidmouth safe – will you take charge of that, Norman? Good, we can leave that to you, then. Perhaps we should all listen to what Lionel Sharpe has to tell us now. I've already shared some of the contents of your coded cable with Alex and Melpomene and Jimmy Manley, Lionel. Would you like to tell us what else you think will be valuable at this stage of our enquiries, now you have heard what Alastair has had to say? And maybe you have some questions of us, as you have only just met everyone and plenty has been happening while you were enjoying your luxurious banana-boat cruise on the way here from St Luke."

Lionel Sharpe laughed at this, "The Santa Katalina is hardly up to Cunard standard, but I can't complain. I certainly played a lot of bridge en route! If she is willing, maybe Melpomene could relate everything I've missed, including letting me know about my dear daughter's recent exploits. By the way, I shall telephone my wife this evening and persuade her to join us as soon as a passage can be arranged."

As requested, Mel narrated the whole story, including her defeat of her kidnapper, Marie-Colette's own escape from captivity, Elizabeth O'Connor's murder and finally Douglas' failed attempt to murder his own wife, and Alastair's enterprise in foiling that.

She finished by saying, "Lionel, you have probably been told that at the end of today, you will be given into the care of Eugenie and Stephen Buckmaster and reunited with Janice there. It is understood you might still be a target, so precautions will be taken. With any luck we shall soon be able to mop up the rest of the gang – at least, the English branch of the cabal. As for the continental sections, we shall have to take advice from Hugo Palance, when he arrives, which should be this afternoon, with any luck."

"Thankyou for that, Melpomene – you have apparently all had a very entertaining time while I have been lazing on board ship! Now I'll bring everyone up to date with what I discovered before I left St Luke. As you will have guessed, Brigadier Douglas had a very active trade going on, mainly between the St Luke Embassy here in London and the British Embassy in St Luke, but also in significant quantities with diplomatic posts in the Bahamas and Jamaica. From England and France the diplomatic bags carried small-arms and strong liquors to the Caribbean, and the opposite flow was, as you might expect, currency and some small quantities of gold bullion."

He was about to continue when he was interrupted by the entrance of Hugo Palance, looking very happy. He came and kissed Melpomene as usual, and was then introduced to those he had not met, Howard Anderson and, of course, Lionel Sharpe. He said, "Taffy Evans is not coming today – his leg is playing up again – but I have some news which, I think will be very welcome. I decided that matters were coming to a head, and that it was now time to gather in the French arm, so I triggered a plan we at the Sûreté have been preparing for some months now. In a coordinated series of actions, we raided two establishments in Calais – one that might be called the headquarters of the organization and the other which we have been suspecting is their main warehouse. My men were well-prepared and I'm told that only one or two individuals made their escape by using a fast speedboat permanently moored at the warehouse dock – we do not as yet know who they were, but I suspect that such precautions would not have been wasted on minor figures of the cabal."

Lionel Sharpe was very interested, "Tell me, M Palance, did your men get their hands on Henri Mercier, or was he one of those who fled by water?"

"I have not been given his name, so he might well been one of that pair. I am expecting a series of coded cables to be sent to your office, Adrian, so we will know before long who we have scooped up and who we have missed."

Chapter 45

Lionel Sharpe said he, too would be interested to hear who were safely in the bag, and added, "The mention of a speedboat reminds me that on at least one occasion recently, I had information that such a craft was used to convey liquor from Calais to one of the Channel Islands – Guernsey if I remember correctly – for trans-shipment to a merchant vessel sailing under a flag of convenience whose destination was the Bahamas. Would it not be worthwhile, Sir Adrian, to alert your colleagues there to be on the lookout for this boat?"

"Splendid notion, Lionel, we have good relations with the Channel Island police forces. I'll telephone my office right away and they will get onto this!"

For the next hour or so, Lionel Sharpe reported other happenings and other messages he had intercepted, and the general discussion was lively. Winnie, by now had filled two shorthand notebooks and was starting on a third, and said, "I will have about a week's worth of typing once I get back to Crabbe and Crabbe!"

Then a servant appeared and announced that dinner was served in the private dining-room, so everyone drifted there.

Melpomene made a point of sitting next to Lionel Sharpe, and began by relating Janice's experiences to him, not all of which Lionel had heard. Lionel was very interested, of course, and said how pleased he was with the initiative of Phoebe Buckmaster in engaging Crabbe and Crabbe to deal with her friend's problem, saying, "Not many girls of fourteen would have been so enterprising – and I applaud Janice's escape from Hillyard House, too, though that might sound an irresponsible attitude for a father!"

Meanwhile, Alex had seated himself between Alastair Robson and Jimmy Manley, saying, "How shall we play our visit to the Builders Arms tomorrow? Is it one of the usual nights for your companions to meet, Alastair? – I don't suppose it happens every day, does it?"

"Luckily, tomorrow is in fact a regular evening for our gatherings. I have been wondering how I shall identify suitable candidates – I think I can recognize likely villains, but I shall need some burly policemen to do the actual arresting. I would rather keep under cover for as long as possible, so I don't want to appear involved in that."

Said Jimmy, "You could use the 'Judas kiss' approach, Alastair! Not actually kissing, of course, but you could arrange to touch or speak to those you wished to be singled out, while avoiding direct contact with others, while someone watches and takes notes. Then those you have 'kissed' could be arrested as they leave the bar, or some similar arrangement could be worked out."

"Melpomene actually has some experience of keeping surveillance in a pub while pretending to be there for some other reason," said Alex, "perhaps we should talk to her later – she appears to be busy with Lionel Sharpe at the moment. Where could we all meet, maybe tomorrow afternoon, to plan our approach? We will have to be careful not to blow your cover, of course, Alastair – by the way, where have you been staying since you grabbed Douglas? And I've been meaning to ask, is Leonie Douglas being taken care of somewhere? Mel was going to ask Walter Huskisson whether he knew, but I don't think she's had a chance yet."

"You might not credit this, but I have been staying with my Mum and Dad, off the beaten track in Walthamstow – they are under the impression that I have always been pursuing the duties of an ordinary detective-sergeant, but not attached to any particular station. I've stayed with them before, in between my under-cover activities, and they no longer bother to ask me what I've been up to lately. Mum's cooking suits me better than what I was offered in the servants' quarters of the Douglas establishment, and she has never tried to poison me, either!"

After the meal, Adrian Fitz-Hugh announced that those who wished to stay overnight would be accommodated for no charge – however nobody opted for this. He also announced that there were additional cars and drivers available, so people need not feel that they had to go home by the same means and route that they had arrived. "Howard and Hugo Palance will be coming with me, and Jimmy is taking care of getting Alastair Robson home, I'm told."

Melpomene suggested to Lionel Sharpe that he might feel like coming to stay at the Crabbe and Crabbe flat that night – he gratefully accepted, saying that he had brought an overnight bag with him off the boat at Gravesend, while the remainder of his baggage was being carried on to Tilbury. Winnie would accompany them, of course, to be dropped of at her digs.

"Then," said Mel, "we can work out the best way of getting you to Stephen and Eugenie Buckmaster's – Janice will be there soon, and it would not be a good idea for you to go to the school yet, I would say, since we don't know how much the people there know."

When the driver pulled up at Winnie's digs, the exhausted secretary had to be woken up. "Are we there already?" she asked, "It seems only five minutes since we left – how nice it is to travel in a big, warm, comfortable limousine for a change! Not that I dislike your Riley, Mel and Alex!" "No offence taken!" said Melpomene, "see you in the office tomorrow morning – not quite sure when. Nighty night, sleep tight!"

When they got to the flat, Caroline and Mrs M had already retired, but had thought to make sure that the spare bedroom was made up. Lionel Sharpe was also rather keen to get to bed, so after a cup of chocolate and a quick bath he turned in, saying, "How pleasant to bathe in fresh water with proper soap! It was all sea-water on the Santa Katalina!"

Straight after breakfast, the telephoning began. Alex got onto Mile End Road to discover if there was any more news of captured villains, while Melpomene called the hospital to enquire about Desmond McPhail. Alex drew a blank, Jimmy saying that it mainly depended now on what could be found out from Alastair's contacts at the Builders Arms, so Lionel asked whether he could phone his wife in St Luke, saying that it would be late at night there, but he might catch her.

Melpomene had more luck. The report from the hospital was quite encouraging, Desmond was now awake and only lightly sedated, and X-rays had shown that the internal wounds were healing well. The collapsed lung had been re-inflated and was functioning as well as could be expected.

Lionel was unable to telephone his wife, but said that he had expected this and would try again later in the day. Then Melpomene suggested he ring the Buckmasters to let them know when he would be joining them later. He spoke to Stephen, who then said, "You will be pleased to know that your wife is already on board a Cunard vessel, which will reach Southampton in less than a week!"

Chapter 46

Lionel, of course was very pleased to hear this news, and asked, "Do you know the name of the ship, Stephen? I can look up the shipping news in the newspapers, then, and get the latest information about when she will be docking. I can hardly wait! Poor Janice will be on tenterhooks until we see her, too!"

"The ship is the Carinthia – she is usually in service on the Canada run but is engaged in cruising at the moment, so will pick up her passengers in Jamaica, I'm told, before crossing the Atlantic. Your wife will no doubt have an interesting story to relate – the ship is likely to be more comfortable than the Santa Katalina, by all accounts!"

Alex then suggested they ought to plan their visit to the Builders Arms that evening. "I meant to ask Jimmy for Alastair's telephone number when I was talking to him before – I'll ring Mile End Road again."

Jimmy told him the number, but then said, "More news about assorted crooks! We ran fingerprint checks on the car used by Desmond's assailants. Of course they were mostly those of the owner, Mr Morgan, and various other people – we had taken his prints when we told him that we had his car in our yard – but we did find a clear set of left thumb and index finger on the passenger's side window, which we then put through our records just in case, and these proved to be interesting! I won't go into it now, but we classify prints on the basis of several visible features, and we found a match with enough of them to make it worthwhile proceeding further, especially as the owner of the probable match had been inside on a charge of malicious wounding with a fire-arm, to wit, a revolver!"

"Was there anything valuable to be found from the bullets they dug out of poor Desmond?" asked Alex.

"In fact, there was only one to be found – the other had gone clean through, there was a definite exit wound on his back! I've got a young detective scratching through the area around Desmond's front gate for it, but I'm not raising my hopes! We've done a microscopic analysis of the one we did find, so we'll be in a good position to match it with any gun that turns up. It's a 9 by 19 mm Parabellum, the round used in Luger pistols like yours, Alex, as well as in some others. Lugers seem popular with these gentry, the pistols we took off the two who tried it on with Madame Huskisson were both Lugers, as was the one that Melpomene seized from her foiled kidnapper. And, interestingly, they had almost consecutive serial numbers, so might have come from the same production batch. I'm thinking that these crooks may have kept one of the consignments destined for running to the Bahamas for their own use."

When Jimmy rang off, Alex tried Alastair's number. The telephone was answered by someone he took for Alastair's Mum, who said that he was off somewhere on business, she didn't know exactly where, "He never tells us, because he says it's better for me and Dad not to know – he does very important work, you understand! But I think he was going by tube, because his motorbike is still in the shed."

Alex thanked her and said, "If you see him again and he asks, tell him Alex rang and that we shall be at our office."

Then they all got in the Riley and drove there, to discover Winnie furiously typing away on her notes from the previous day. "Where's Marjorie?" Mel asked, "Oh, she's popped out for some essentials," said Winnie, "we had nearly run out of Lapsang Souchong, and the corner shop doesn't keep it. I expect she will bring jam tarts too, and she said she would get something particularly nice, as we will have visitors later – Alastair Robson rang and said he would be here shortly, and I thought you would be likely to bring Colonel Sharpe."

"As soon as she is back," said Mel, "we'll have cups of tea and whatever delicacy she has bought, and then we'll talk about our visit to the pub this evening."

Alastair having arrived, Lionel was brought up to date about the programme of regimental reunions at the Builders Arms. He asked, "How will you know which men are simply old soldiers wanting to cling on nostalgically to a spirit of comradeship, and which are gang members?"

Alastair pointed out that this was indeed difficult, "Some of them I know about for sure, because I actually worked with them on various illicit activities – I must even admit to helping crimes to be committed sometimes, though I can salve my conscience by convincing myself that these delinquents would be brought to account in due course. Mostly these known men formed part of a separate clique who were directed by someone who we called 'the adjutant' and drew together to execute the duties he would hand out. I can, of course point him out when I see him, as well as those directly involved. It would be tempting to round them all up at once, but this might effectively spoil any other lines of enquiry we might want to pursue by warning off associated gangs, particularly those from other countries. We know that there are French chapters in the main cabal. Melpomene will tell us what she has in mind for this evening."

Melpomene said, "Thanks, Alastair. First I have a question – I believe that these meetings are held in the saloon bar of the pub. Is this reserved solely for the regimental people, or do other customers use the room? In particular, is it usual to see any women there on those nights?"

"Good question, Mel!" replied Alastair, "By the way, remember that I'm Ted Hinchcliffe in that company! Yes, the general public is free to use the bar those nights, and there are often several women there, both respectable ladies with their husbands or friends and those looking for prey!"

"So I'd better make sure I dress in such a way that I cannot be mistaken for the latter! What I might do – please let me know what you think, everyone – is this. I will go in by myself, although Alex might want to settle himself in a corner to keep an eye on proceedings. As I did a while ago when we were observing customers for another case, I shall take in a copy of The Times, folded back to the crossword page, and I will work on the crossword while enjoying a drink. This will give me a reason for being there and allow me to watch and make notes – if anyone bothers they will think I'm working out anagrams or something – I'll have to limit my speed, I can usually knock off the Times cryptic in twenty minutes or so!"

"Meanwhile, Alastair – sorry, Ted – will make a point of touching whoever he talks to who he knows to be a villain, while avoiding such contact with others. I shall make such shorthand notes – of clothes, physical distinguishing features and so on – as will be adequate for later identification."

"And when we have fingered as many as possible," went on Alastair, "Mel will put her newspaper down and go to the bar for a fill-up. Then, Jimmy will pick it up and go outside to meet his team, including WDC Jennifer Sweet, who will quickly make herself familiar with Mel's list of descriptions. Then it will simply be a question of waiting for closing time!"

Chapter 47

Melpomene wondered what else they all needed to get done before their excursion to the Builders Arms in the evening, "There must be things on our list that we haven't got round to yet, let's try and think. I must admit to being in quite a whirl lately. Alex, do you need to check with Walter Huskisscn – didn't we say that we ought to make sure that there was nobody at the embassy still at risk?"

"You're right, Mel, I'll ring him now. It should be OK to use his embassy number, now we've cleaned the place up a bit!"

Alex was soon talking to Walter, and motioned to Mel to pick up the second ear-piece, to hear Walter saying, "I've just had a long session with HE the Ambassador, Chevalier de Chapelle. He summoned me to his office and asked me if I could please explain to him just what has been going on – he had been told about the death of Elizabeth O'Connor, the attempt to kidnap Marie-Colette, and the shooting of Desmond McPhail, but he was not yet aware that Brigadier Douglas had been arrested, and knew nothing about his threats to Mrs Douglas. So I made a clean breast of it all, starting by telling him about the reasons for my original approach to Detective-Inspector Manley and my subsequent dealings with Crabbe and Crabbe. He listened patiently and when I had finished, he clasped my hand warmly and told me that he was very grateful to me and my associates, saying that he had been over-reluctant to take action when he first became suspicious of Douglas. And he went on to ask me to set up a meeting with you and Melpomene, plus Jimmy Manley and perhaps Sir Howard Anderson from the FO, as soon as possible, maybe tomorrow, in his suite at the embassy. I got the feeling that he felt it was high time for him to get properly involved!"

Melpomene took the telephone from Alex and told Walter that she would be delighted to participate, and asked him to suggest that Alastair Robson be invited, too.

"And there's something else, Walter," she added, "I reckon that Desmond was shot because the crooks knew he had been gathering information about illicit transactions at the embassy. He told us that he had started to compile a dossier on Douglas and Elizabeth O'Connor, and I'm wondering where that dossier is now. Desmond would have been very careful to keep it somewhere secure, not just in his office with his other documents, so we should take steps to make sure it is still safe. I feel reluctant to bother Desmond about it until he is completely recovered, but maybe I'll telephone Morag McPhail – he might have told her about it."

"There's something else, Mel," said Walter, "you may remember that my first suspicions about illegal dealings were prompted by a colleague's sudden acquisition of a pair of beautiful hand-made boots. I don't think I ever told you his name, but I will now, so that if it turns up in the dossier or otherwise you will be able to make the connection. His name is Keith Hogan, he is one of my staff in Commerce. I have been watching him since the episode of the boots, but have noticed nothing further to cause me concern. While I mention it, I recall telling you about another colleague who had just bought a villa at Southend-on-Sea – well this turns out to have been a false alarm – in fact the place was inherited. So I'm rather glad I never mentioned his name! Give my regards to Morag if you reach her – I believe she is spending quite a lot of time at the hospital."

When she had hung up the telephone, Melpomene said, "None of your usual quips, please, Alex, but I can feel lunchtime coming on – shall we go to Guiseppe's? How about you girls?"

"I've got my Mum's cut lunch as usual, thank you, Mel" said Marjorie, "How about you, Winnie?"

"Oh, I shall carry on with the typing – I'll pop down to the shop later and get something, don't worry!"

At the trattoria, the pair and Alastair and Lionel had no difficulty selecting something delicious, so they were soon tucking in and chatting.

"Before I forget again," said Alastair, "I should remind you that your Riley is known to the gang – remember that the note to Mel's kidnapper mentioned the fact that it was a tourer – so it would not be a good idea to park it anywhere near the pub tonight. Fortunately, Mel, you have since disposed of your blonde curls, so you might not be as easily recognized as you were then."

"Yes, I'm going to make sure my new brown locks are visible," said Mel, "and I shall lay on the make-up a bit more than I do usually, being careful not to go so far that I look like a lady of the night! Another thing – you had Jimmy as part of the pub scenario, Alastair – are you sure that he is not known to the gang – there are likely to be habituals in the group, who might have had their collars felt by Jimmy in the past!"

"Good point, Mel! Perhaps we had better leave Alex to pick up the newspaper and take it outside for Jennifer Sweet to interpret. Jimmy can be with his men in the shadows waiting to pounce, there is no need for them to announce themselves."

Alex said, "I have no idea whether or not I'm known to these people. Mel has fun disguising herself, so I might do likewise. When I was pretending to be a gas inspector, I just omitted to shave as well as wearing a suitable outfit – any suggestions, Alastair, as an experienced under-cover operative?"

"Yes, Alex! My suggestion is that unless you are going to enlist the services of a professional, I wouldn't attempt anything – all you will do with false moustaches or wigs and so on is to make yourself conspicuous. The main thing is to adopt the right attitude of mind and tell yourself that you always go to a saloon bar for a drink in the evenings and that you are very comfortable there!"

Lionel Sharpe had been listening intently to the conversation, and made a suggestion, "I understand that the people in question here are mainly ex-servicemen, so another thing you should avoid doing, Alex, is to try to fit into their world by joining in with their conversations. Just sit back and listen if you like, but if they address you, be as non-committal as you can. Old soldiers develop an even stronger esprit de corps once they are out of the service than when they were still in, and if they feel anyone is trying to interlope, this could get their backs up. Alastair has probably already established his bona fides with these men. By the way, were you in the service, Alastair?"

"Yes, but what I'm very careful not to let on is that I was in the Military Police! That fine body of men is not particularly popular with regimental soldiers! But at least, I am familiar with soldiers' language and attitudes, so I'm not likely to commit any faux pas!"

"Let us talk some more back at the office," said Alex, "but this lunchtime conversation has got us in the right mood for this evening, I'm sure!"

Chapter 48

During the afternoon everyone took the opportunity to familiarize themselves with the notes from Crowminster Hall, which Winnie had finished typing, with two carbon copies.

Melpomene said, "I had better telephone Jimmy Manley and make sure we are all singing from the same score this evening. I don't imagine he will have missed anything, but we have changed the arrangements a little. And I'll tell him about the Ambassador's meeting, too – Walter has negotiated for it to be held at 1 p.m."

She confirmed this with Jimmy, and then he said he had some more news, "Desmond is sitting up now, and taking a little nourishment, so Morag asked him about the dossier. He had, as we thought, taken it home with him and it is safely stowed in their wardrobe. He reckons that its main value will be as evidence at any trials that come up, he doesn't think there is much in it that we don't already know. Anyway, it can wait. But I can tell you that we have made some more identifications, Mel, so let Alastair listen on the other earpiece – he might be interested in this!"

Mel told Alastair, and he picked it up. "Alastair's listening now, Jimmy, go ahead!" Mel told him.

"I told you we'd picked up a set of prints from the car used in the assassination attempt on Desmond – it has given us a definite ID on a likely perpetrator, a bloke by the name of Dudley Hargreaves, who did time a while back for aggravated assault – apparently he threatened a tobacconist he was trying to rob, by waving a pistol at him. At the time he was accompanied by an Abel Stinson, who got off due to insufficient evidence. What's more, they are both former members of the Rutland Light Infantry!"

Alastair exclaimed, "I know both of these characters – they always go around together – I'd lay any money you like that they are the ones who shot Desmond! If they're at the pub tonight, I'll certainly finger them!"

Jimmy went on, "I heard that! But they'll probably be laying low now. There's more, but it can wait, too. One more thing about tonight. I've selected four men to help me with the nabbing, and we'll be in an unmarked van just down the street. And I shall station a pair of uniformed PCs on the other side of the pub entrance, who will peer at everyone to induce those with guilty consciences to come our way. There'll probably be a stream of customers leaving the pub at closing time, so Jennifer Sweet is going to stand outside the door, looking as though she's waiting for someone – which she will be, of course! – and she will tip us the wink as she spots the ones on Melpomene's list. Even if we only grab one or two, the effort will be worth it!"

"Best of luck for tonight, Jimmy!" said Mel, "We probably won't get a chance to talk to you again until the dust has settled. We are going to travel by tube after all, it's only a short walk to the pub, and this will avoid the car being recognized. See you tomorrow at the Ambassador's place at one o'clock."

That evening all went to plan for a while. Alastair was greeted as he got a beer at the counter by a man sporting a handlebar moustache, who sang out, "Hello, Hinch, long time no see!" He replied. "Evening, Adj – I've been busy elsewhere!" shook his hand, went with him to a table in the corner, and joined the three others already there. He nodded to one, shook hands with another and patted the third companionably on the shoulder. Mel, seated across the room with her port and lemon, made rapid notes on the margin of her paper.

After another half an hour or so, two more men came into the bar and headed toward that table, but when on the way there they spotted Alex, hesitated and looked hard at each other. They then collected some drinks and went to join the others. Alastair shook both their hands, and they sat down and joined in with the conversation.

Not much happened for the next hour or so, and by that time closing time was approaching, so Mel went and bought herself another drink at the bar – gin and orange this time, having found port and lemon too sweet for her taste. Alex, who had been sitting reading a motoring magazine over two or three beers, rose, said "Goodnight!" to the barman, wandered over and picked up Mel's Times and left the bar. But as he did, the two latecomers nudged one another and stood and followed him out.

They caught up with him as he stood at the door waiting for some eager customers to push their way in, took him by each arm and hustled him out onto the street. The taller of the two drew a pistol from a shoulder-holster, thrust it into his chest and growled at him. "Not so fast, Mr Crabbe, we've got some questions for you first!"

Then he saw the two uniformed policemen starting toward them, and while he hesitated, Jimmy Manley came up from behind and knocked his gun arm up. The pistol went off, but harmlessly, except for the plate-glass front window of an adjacent shoe-shop, which shattered spectacularly all over the pavement. With all this distraction, the two bewildered would-be assailants were soon overpowered and cuffed, relieved of their pistols, and bundled off into the waiting van.

The shot, of course, had seized the attention of the patrons who were by now streaming out of the saloon bar, so in the confusion, WDC Jennifer Sweet was only able to point out the moustachioed adjutant, who was soon handcuffed and joining the others in the van.

"Ah well!" said Jimmy to Melpomene, who had joined them, "Three notorious villains is not a bad score for one evening! What's the betting that we have just grabbed Hargreaves and Stinson as well as the so-called adjutant?"

"I must say I am relieved that they didn't spot me too!" said Melpomene, "I can thank you for that, Jimmy, if I had my natural blonde curls still, I would have been easy meat! I suppose they will all be hurled into the choky and charged now?"

"Yes, Mel, we'll hold them on a charge of going armed in company with intent to commit a felony – the adjutant was carrying a Luger as well. There will be a raft of other charges later, of course, when we put all the evidence together. By the way, you and Alex and Alastair were all, strictly speaking, going armed in company too – the important difference being that, as far as I know, you had no intention to commit an offence!"

Back at the flat, they reported all that had happened to Lionel Sharpe, drank some calming cups of chocolate, bathed and went to bed.

"Don't wake me too early!" said Melpomene, "I need to sleep in until at least 8.30!"

"You had better leave a note for Caroline, then!" said Alex.

Chapter 49

When she finally awoke, Melpomene said, "I really need to have my hair restored to its original colour and curliness, especially as we are to meet the Ambassador today. I'll ring Jimmy or Jennifer Sweet and get the number of that hairdresser, Lucy Stafford."

"Won't it be in the book?" asked Alex. "Maybe not, I don't know if the name of the salon is the same as hers. I'll try, anyway, I imagine Jimmy and Jennifer will be busy this morning."

As it happened, Mel found the number easily and made an appointment, telling Lucy, "I really need to be ready before I go to an important meeting at one o'clock." Lucy assured her that if she came in before eleven she could restore her original appearance in plenty of time. And indeed so she did, so that a newly refurbished Mel, with Alex and Lionel drew up in the Riley at the embassy at ten to one, to find Jimmy and Alastair already waiting in the foyer. An attendant told them, "Sir Howard Anderson has already gone up, come with me, please."

His Excellency welcomed them cordially and introduced his wife, Madame Héloïse de Chapelle, the head of chancery, M Marcel Lavalier, and the chief of protocol, M Alain du Pont, as well as Walter Huskisson, "Who most of you know already!" He continued, "Mr Sidmouth, the comptroller, is otherwise engaged at the moment, largely on the basis of information supplied by Desmond McPhail and Colonel Sharpe," and then chuckled, "as Detective-Inspector Manley is already aware, the embassy books are currently being audited by Mr Philip Seaward, the principal of an independent accountancy firm in the City, who has already discovered a number of irregularities, and Sidmouth has been called in so that he can attempt to justify them. I need not tell this company that this is a matter of extreme confidentiality!"

He went on, "Before we get down to business, ladies and gentlemen, I would like to offer a toast to Walter Huskisson, Jimmy Manley and Melpomene and Alex Crabbe, who have so far been of inestimable value to this Embassy and therefore to the state of St Luke as a whole, and look like continuing this service over the weeks and months to come. To your good health, my friends! Now I would like each member of my staff, starting with Walter, to present a personal view of the events of recent months."

When these accounts were over, taking a couple of hours, M de Chapelle called for reactions and qualifications from the investigative team, which were found to be mainly details of a minor nature, and then said, "I hope the notice will not be too short as to cause you any inconvenience, but I would now like to invite all of you present, as well as the two Crabbe and Crabbe secretaries, and the key members of Inspector Manley's staff, to a reception and banquet that my wife and I are arranging for two days from now, at seven o'clock, in the grand dining hall of our Embassy. Please say you can all come – I would like to make a special event of this!"

After these formal proceedings, attendants circulated with canapés and champagne as well as mineral water for those who needed to drive. Both Mel and Alex declined the champagne, explaining that they had taken alcohol as a matter of business the day before!

As they walked down the grand staircase on the way out, Lionel asked Mel and Alex whether he might take the opportunity the next day to go to Tilbury and pick up his baggage. "No need!" said Alex, "If I telephone my friend Senior Preventive Officer Ben Fisher, I'm sure he would only be too glad to arrange that for you. Furthermore, if you would like it forwarded to the Buckmasters in Woodhampton, I'm sure that would be possible, too. This brings up the question of when you would like to pick up Janice from school. One or both of us can drive you to Hillyard House tomorrow, if you like – you have been very undemanding so far, and we haven't had a decent drive lately!"

Lionel was very pleased, "Thank you very much – I will take you up on that, Alex!"

Back at the flat, they discovered that Mrs M, not knowing exactly when they would return, had prepared a meal of spaghetti all'arrabbiata, which she rendered as 'spaghetti all rabbits' ("Though it ain't got no rabbits in it – but Eyetalians are strange, anyway!"). Whatever you called it, it was very tasty!

The next morning saw them driving down the Brighton Road, the weather being one of those late Autumn days which are so pleasant, although they presage the cold that is to come before Christmas.

At the school they were taken in to see Sister Boniface, who greeted them warmly, "Janice has been so anxious to see you, Colonel! I understand you are going to be staying with the Buckmasters until your wife arrives – will you take Phoebe home with you today? The girls are in class at the moment, but I warned matron that they would need their trunks checked – we don't want the usual collection of wet towels and miscellaneous underwear that girls often leave behind. Will you have a cup of tea before you go to Woodhampton?"

"While we're waiting, Colonel Sharpe and Mr and Mrs Crabbe, I might mention that we have been pestered weekly by Mr Ogilvie, who wants us to let him take his daughter away. Of course I have flatly refused and Major Buckmaster has backed me up on this. I have given everybody here firm instructions that if he turns up the police must be informed immediately. Unfortunately we have been unable to telephone Mrs Edith Grantley, Lucy's grandmother, otherwise I would ask her to take Lucy away to somewhere safe."

"Sister," said Melpomene, "am I right in assuming that Major Buckmaster is Lucy's legal guardian? If so, we could take her to Woodhampton with the two other girls."

"Very good thinking, Mrs Crabbe! Let me telephone the Buckmasters and see whether they agree – otherwise I shall have to keep her here over the Christmas holidays!"

She picked up the telephone and talked to the switch, "Can you get me Mrs or Major Buckmaster in Woodhampton, please, Edith? Ah, Eugenie, Florence Boniface here – would young Lucy Ogilvie be welcome at your place until we can locate Mrs Grantley? Is Major Buckmaster in a position to pick up Lucy, Phoebe and Janice Sharpe and her father this afternoon? If not, I can ask Mr and Mrs Crabbe to bring them. You will both come? – Wonderful, we'll see you soon."

Soon the three girls were brought, Lionel and Janice embraced warmly and both Janice and Phoebe hugged and kissed Melpomene and hugged Alex. Lucy was a little bewildered, but spoke up happily when the arrangements were explained to her. Alex and Melpomene made their departure, thanking Sister Boniface for being so understanding.

Chapter 50

On the drive back to London, Melpomene tried to work out what remained to be done before the reception, first saying, "You know, Alex, now that Desmond is sitting up and taking notice, we ought to visit him in hospital, both to support him and to let him know that we have caught the two who tried to do away with him. Is he at the Finchley hospital? Maybe we should call in on the way home."

"Very well, Mel, we'll do that. And the other matter I have in mind is to get the latest updates on identifications, arrests and charges laid for the members of the opposition. Jimmy will be the best one to ask, of course."

At the hospital they asked to see Desmond McPhail, and were directed to a private ward, where they found Desmond, looking reasonably well, playing court to Morag, little Phillipa and Jimmy Manley. Melpomene presented him with the statutory bunch of grapes, and said, "You are looking quite good, Desmond, when do you expect to go home? I suppose Jimmy has already told you that your would-be murderers have been rounded up."

"Yes, and he has also told me that Cyril Sidmouth is currently being interrogated under bright lights – which brings me, I must say, a comfortable feeling of schadenfreude. Many of the entries about him in my dossier, which Morag has promised to pass on to Jimmy, will, I think, be useful evidence when Sidmouth is charged with embezzlement and other offences!"

After more conversation, Mel and Alex took their leave. Mel was driving now, and went straight to the office. She ran up the stairs and said to Marjorie and Winnie, "Alex will mind the shop – we three are off to Bond Street, where I'm going to buy you both glamorous dresses for the reception this evening! I'm going to wear my new gold dress with the sheer overlay, so I don't want you two to be outshone! See you later, Alex – I hope your tails are properly ironed and your patent shoes well shined! Ring Caroline and make sure, my darling."

The shopping expedition was successful and the two secretaries were very pleased and grateful, "Don't mention it!" said Mel, "You two deserve to be properly recognized for all the support, over and above the call of duty, that you have given the firm on this case!"

"By the way," said Marjorie, "I took an enquiry this morning that might interest you both – but I didn't know whether you were free yet, so I told the caller I would have to check and get back to him."

"Oh, we're free all right!" said Alex, "It's over to Jimmy and his people now! What was it about?"

"It was from a Doctor Gordon Salmon at the emergency department of Finchley Hospital. He said you might remember him from the time when you took in the guy who Melpomene shot in the hand. He said that he was getting worried about possible shenanigans in the hospital pharmacy. I have his number, should I try it now?"

Salmon was busy when they called, but would call back when he was free. The telephone rang after fifteen minutes or so, and Alex took the call, with Mel listening on the other earpiece.

"Gordon Salmon here, sorry for the delay, but I was overseeing the splinting and plastering of someone's leg that had come off second best in an argument with a milk float! I'm concerned about two matters here at the hospital, the first to do with the pharmacy, and the second a series of complaints that patients have lost possessions and cash. The latter is obviously no concern of the medical staff, but all the same, I have felt uneasy about the way that the hospital administration has been dealing with it. I have spoken to them, but – you probably wouldn't have come across this – there is often a serious climate of suspicion between the two sides in a hospital, so my remarks were largely discounted. I have come to believe that this thievery is not casual, but organized by a dishonest group of staff. As for the pharmacy matter, I have also come to believe that this amounts to a commercial business run from within the hospital, supplying all manner of medicines, including drugs of addiction, to an outside gang. Either of these worries is beyond my own power to investigate – besides, I have my time cut out fulfilling my medical duties! Would you be willing to have a poke around here?"

"This could indeed be interesting to us, Dr Salmon – I will talk to my partner about it – the rest of today is out, I'm afraid. Can I get back to you tomorrow?"

"Good, Alex, we'll pick it up tomorrow, "said Melpomene, "right now we need to have lunch and then go home to get ready for tonight. Are you two girls going home, now? Shall we pick you up to go to the embassy, say at twenty to seven?"

"Yes, Mel," said Marjorie, "Winnie is going to come home with me now, so we can get ready together, and help each other with our hair and make-up! See you at my place then!"

They all arrived at the embassy in good time, and were taken to the grand dining room, where the ambassador was waiting, with outstretched arms, "Speeches and formalities first," he announced, "and then we can relax and enjoy ourselves!"

"Ladies and gentlemen!" he said, "first, I am going to express the appreciation of the embassy and of our country. Would Marjorie Wentworth and Winifred Morris please step forward."

From an attendant, he took two flat packages, which he handed to the two secretaries, saying, "Open them please, and perhaps one of you could read one out to the assembly."

Winifred unwrapped hers, to disclose a framed certificate. "This is very impressive!" she said, "There is a beautiful coat of arms and then it says, 'Presented to Miss Winifred Morris, in gratitude for her services to the embassy and state of St Luke', and the date and signature. Oh, thank you Your Excellency, this will look wonderful on the office wall, next to Marjorie's!"

There was applause from everyone there, and the ambassador said, "Now would Melpomene and Alex step forward, please." He was handed a silver medallion on a royal-blue ribbon, which he placed around Mel's neck, followed by a similar one for Alex.

"These are the medals of the Order of Saint Luke – they are each accompanied by a scroll, which the recipients can read at their leisure, since they are drafted in Latin! Only four of these orders have been bestowed over the past twenty-five years, since Independence! Now, ladies and gentlemen, let the festivities commence!"

He led Mel to sit on his left, with Alex on Madame de Chapelle's right, and a line of waiters started bringing the first course, a cold vegetarian consommé, in deference to the Huskissons. "But there will be free choices, later!" said Héloïse.

FIN

KEEP VIGILANT FOR THE NEXT CASE!

Crabbe and Crabbe's next case will be coming out soon!

Will there be murders? Who knows.

Will there be skullduggery? Undoubtedly.

Will Melpomene and Alex solve the case?

Of course – how could anyone doubt this!

Look out for:

"A Medical Emergency"

A Case for Crabbe and Crabbe.

By Geoffrey Foster

Coming in a few months.

www.ingramcontent.com/pod-product-compliance
Lightning Source LLC
Chambersburg PA
CBHW052141170626
46812CB00004B/1533